Somebody is Killing the Trophy Wives of Beverly Hills

John Kane

BooksForABuck.com
2012

This is a work of fiction. All characters, events, and locations are fictitious or used fictitiously. Any resemblance to actual events or people is coincidental.

BooksForABuck.com
August 2012
ISBN: 978-1-60215-180-2

"A woman who does not wear perfume has no future."

Coco Chanel

"Big girls need big diamonds."

Elizabeth Taylor

1

People say if life hands you lemons, make lemonade. I say if life hands you olives, make a dirty martini. If you're given an opportunity, make the most of it. Don't just stick that olive on a toothpick and use it as an appetizer. Surround it with some top shelf gin, a splash of olive juice, then sit back, relax, and start sipping.

I'm Nikki Tyler and if you don't know me, then you must not have taken a plane lately. After all, my books are in every airport in America, right next to the Cinnabuns. In fact, I like to think of my books as literary Cinnabuns, fast food treats pumped up with melodrama and drizzled with a thick icing of sex. They may not be good for you, but they're hard to resist and perfect for a direct flight from Dallas to New York. Reviewing my last book, "The Girl from Oz," the totally fictional account of a young Australian actress who marries an American superstar, divorces him over a cult religion, and then finds happiness in the arms of hunky country singer, *People Magazine* referred to me as "the Jane Austen of the orgasm."

Like everyone else in this town, I started out as an actress, but you really can't earn yourself much more than a condo in West Hollywood when you're doing direct to video thrillers like *Top Gun Nurses* and *Blood Orgy*. So I went into writing about ten years ago, just when the marriage went kaput, and I'm not bashful about saying that I've done quite well for myself.

I write about Hollywood because it's where I live and it's what I know. Besides, everybody wants to know about Hollywood, so if you're selling that, and sex, you've got an audience. Right now I'm slaving away on *Malibu Bad Boy*, the story of an aging action star who ditches his wife, joins an anti-Semitic cult of Holocaust deniers, and then sees the light when he falls in love with a gorgeous Israeli secret agent. Ever wonder where I get my ideas from? (Hey, I make 'em up!)

I'd been working all morning on my big love scene, the first time the hero and the secret agent go to bed, and had just tapped out the following on my trusty old computer: "He entered her softly, thrusting into her and then holding still, his member swelling inside her like a hungry python devouring its prey in one greedy gulp."

"That's it!" I whooped.

"That's what?" inquired my assistant Madison who's all of twenty three, fresh out of Dartmouth and determined to make it in publishing.

When Madison's not working for me, she freelances as a correspondent for *TMZ*, everyone's favorite gossip website.

"I just did it," I said. "Pulled off another of my killer sentences." I love it when it just flows out of me and I see it on the page and know that my readers are going to eat it up with a spoon.

"Let's see." Madison walked over from her desk where she was updating my web site and peered over my shoulder.

"What do you think?"

"Joan Didion is slitting her wrists as we speak."

That's what I love about Madison. She doesn't take my stuff any more seriously than I do. It's entertainment, it's fun, and nobody's getting hurt.

"I'm celebrating." I got up from my chair and grabbed my keys and my purse.

"But Lynn wants to see some pages by the end of the week." Lynn is my editor back in New York, has been ever since I started writing, and I love her. But even she knows a writer needs a break. I'd been in front of the computer all morning and now I wanted lunch. A nice lunch.

"If she calls, tell her I'll be back by three."

"What if she wants to see something?" persisted Madison. These college girls, no sense of humor.

"Send her some pages. Write them yourself!" I grabbed my bag, my Ray Bans and was out the door and into my gold Bentley in a flash. Around noon, it just about directs itself automatically to the Polo Lounge, always my definition of a good lunch and just a few blocks away from my place.

I swung up the driveway of the Beverly Hills Hotel, valeted my car— there's a Los Angeles verb for you—and walked into the lobby. I love the Beverly Hills; it's plush and cozy and old Hollywood. You feel safe there.

I always sit outside on the terrace. It's lovely and private, white wrought iron furniture and fresh flowers on every table. Makes you feel like you're in the South of France. On my way through the indoor dining room I saw Dr. Phil at one table and Jack Black at another. And, sitting in a corner, looking elusive, Mr. Old Hollywood himself, Warren Beatty. There were also some Middle Eastern women, courtesy of all the Saudi money that had come into Beverly Hills in the late eighties. Like the characters in my books, the ladies were all thinly veiled.

Sitting at a center table on the patio was Joel Osmond, whose only relation to Marie was that Nutri System hadn't worked that well for him either. But for sixty plus, Joel was looking pretty good, black turtleneck,

Armani jacket and all his thick silver hair slicked back. Joel and I go all the way back to the late eighties when he produced some of the truly tacky movies I appeared in. He's moved up since then; his most recent film, *Astro Man: Salvation of the Universe* was the second highest grossing film of last year. Joel got his start in show business as a magician in the Bronx; now he can afford to have lunch every day at the Polo Lounge.

"Nikki," he said. "Join us." I noticed he was sitting with his daughter Chloe, always a bit of a problem. Bone thin, her hair wrapped in a Jesse Kamm scarf, Chloe had that sullen look you see on angry young women and hungry Chihuahuas. She'd been daddy's little girl all her life, which had led inevitably to her feeling entitled. Young women in Beverly Hills spoil faster than avocados.

"Joel," I cried, giving him a hug, "you look wonderful. But I just popped in for a bite. Don't want to disturb you."

"I'm leaving soon," announced Chloe. "I have to get back to the shop." Joel had put up the money for a boutique on Robertson that Chloe ran; it carried a bunch of overpriced rags by designers I'd never heard of. It wasn't really a serious business; more of a ploy by Joel to keep Chloe off drugs, which she'd had a long relationship with during her adolescence. In a fit of inspiration, she'd named the place Chlothes.

"Okay." I slipped into the seat next to Joel. "I love those," I said, noticing the gold hoop earrings Chloe was wearing. A small brass monkey hung from each hoop. They actually were pretty jazzy looking.

"Thanks. Just got them in at the store. Drop by and try on a pair."

"She can use the business," added Joel.

I no sooner sat down than the waiter, Javier, was at my side. "What can I get you today, Miss Tyler?"

"I'll have the McCarthy Salad and some passion fruit ice tea. But I want the dressing on the side."

"You never change," he said.

Why should I? The McCarthy salad is the best thing on the menu at the Polo Lounge and, in fact, it's the best salad I've ever eaten. I mean, it's so good, it doesn't even taste like salad. It's just a Cobb salad, but like everything at the Polo Lounge, it's the way they do it. The lettuce is crisp, the chicken freshly broiled, there's wonderful cheddar cheese, and, for a bit of surprise, some chopped beets. I always order the McCarthy salad.

Trying for a good start, I leaned over to Joel and said, "I Netflixed *Astro Man* last week and I adored it. Just adored it."

"Daddy makes movies for the unwashed masses," said Chloe, pushing the food on her plate around like a reluctant seven year old. Borderline anorexia is a hard master.

Joel reached over and patted her hand affectionately. "Those masses help keep me afloat." He loved her; I had to give him that.

"I wish they could help keep me afloat," Chloe sulked. Joel did his best to ignore her, so she turned to me. "Angelina Jolie came in to the store last week."

"What did she buy, a new child?" I asked. That at least got her to smile.

"And so did Leonardo Di Caprio," she continued.

"Chloe gets all the stars," Joel said proudly.

"I always thought I could have had something with Leo," she murmured, her eyes misting over ever so slightly. Somewhere in the distance, I heard the Titanic slowly splitting in two and sinking to the bottom of the Atlantic.

"He's too old for you, sweetheart," said Joel. "You need a guy your age."

"You mean, like the women you marry?" she shot back.

It was no secret that Chloe hated Joel's second wife, Tamara. I never thought it was because Joel divorced her mother, Beverly, for Tamara; more because Chloe felt she had been supplanted. When Beverly and Joel had been married, Chloe was daddy's little girl. That changed when he married Tamara.

The odd thing was, though, that Joel and Tamara had divorced earlier this year. So why was Chloe still bearing a grudge? I couldn't tell by looking at Joel. A producer is a master of pretense; Joel smiled tightly as if his daughter's bitchy remark meant nothing to him.

"Ugh!" Chloe exclaimed, taking a bite of her food and dropping her fork on the table. "This tastes fishy."

"That's because it's tilapia," replied Joel.

Watch out for the salmon, sweetheart, I thought. *It's got fins too.*

"I need to get back," she said, jumping out of her chair. "Thanks for lunch, Daddy."

If Joel was hurt, he hid it under his smile. "I love you, Chloe."

"Me too." She gave him a hug and she was gone.

"She's looking good," I said, trying to apply the gloss.

"It's the heroin."

"Joel!"

"I'm kidding, I'm kidding." He waved his hand in the air. "She hasn't done it for two years now. I'm very proud of her. God knows I've practically underwritten her entire store. She's angry with me now because I won't give her more money for it. I just don't understand why she has to knock Tamara all the time. She knows how much it hurts me."

Joel, Chloe and Tamara all lived in the same household; Tamara in the main house along with Chloe, who had refused to give up her bedroom, and Joel in the pool house in the rear. He was looking for his own place, but not very hard. Wanted to stay close to Tamara, I figured.

"Still carrying the torch?"

Joel stared off into the distance, at the beautiful green lawn that stretched before us, and ignored my question. A man who makes his living as a film producer is not accustomed to telling the truth. He's more likely to feel comfortable shading things to his advantage. A white lie here, an exaggeration there, whatever it takes to make things go his way. Producing movies, like politics, is the art of the possible.

But Joel must have been feeling uncommonly vulnerable today, because he pulled off his reading glasses, rubbed the bridge of his nose and sighed. "I think about her all the time, Nikki."

He looked so vulnerable. I reached out and squeezed his hand. "Oh Joel, that's so sweet. You really loved her."

"Yeah, I did. And she loved me. Until she went crazy this winter and decided to restart her entire life."

Joel and Tamara had met on the set of one of his late 90s epics, *Galaxy Match*, a sci-fi thriller about a wrestling match between an astronaut and an alien. Sylvester Stallone and Mickey Rourke starred in that bit of celluloid immortality; no fair asking which one played the alien. Tamara had a small role as a "space maiden," and spent most of the picture running around in a Mylar bikini. Perfect role for the sweet, spacey blond that was Tamara. Joel fell hard for her. We all thought it was just another mid-life fling, and Beverly, with no pre-nup and the California community property laws that guarantee a wife half her husband's fortune after ten years of marriage, hung tough waiting for Joel to come home. But he never did. I had managed to stay friendly with both Beverly and Tamara, something of prerequisite for living in this community

Joel just looked so sad. "Oh come on, there are lots of other fish in the sea," I said. "It's not all tilapia." That brought a smile. And Javier brought my McCarthy salad, a big, gorgeous green mountain that I dove right into.

9

"We ought to make a film together again," he said.

"Oh Joel, please. There are enough problems in the world!"

"Remember *Bathsheba?*"

Remember it? I'd been trying to forget *Bathsheba, Queen of Blood* for close to two decades now. Demi Moore, right before she hit it big in the Brat Pack, played an ancient lady vampire mistakenly brought back to life by Andrew McCarthy, courtesy of one of those ancient curses that only happen in movies this bad. I played one of Demi's hand maidens, not unlike the space maiden Tamara had played, and the two of us feasted on blood until midway through the picture when Gary Busey slammed a stake through my heart. Roger Ebert actually mentioned me in his notice, but only, I'm sure, because I bared my breasts in the blood sucking scenes. Sadly, *Bathsheba* turns up fairly regularly on AMC.

"Well, I guess you are doing fairly well with the writing," he said.

"I hit twenty million copies this year," I said proudly. "And that's not counting the audio cassettes." Demi, who's a sweetheart and still a friend, had been nice enough to record a few of the audio versions of my books.

"So, since you're so successful, maybe you can give me some advice." Instantly, I sensed a change in the air. Joel the producer, the shaper of the truth, the master manipulator, was back on the scene.

"What would that be?" I asked cautiously.

"Oh, I just thought maybe you could offer some advice to a friend of mine. She's been toying with a book." He was oh so casual, which made my guard go up even higher.

"Toying? Writing is hard work. It's not toying."

"Well of course not. Who would know that better than you? I just thought you could offer some guidance to a first time author."

"Who is she, Joel?" I said, having finished my salad.

"Tamara."

* * * *

Tamara's book arrived the next morning by messenger from Joel's office. I looked at the title page. *Revenge of the Trophy Wives*. Then I looked at the first sentence: "Rain fell on Beverly Hills as twenty year old Amber Biscotti opened her blouse, bared her breasts, and let God's tears wash over her."

Skimming through the first few pages it was clear that Tamara had written a book about all the trout-lipped ladies in town who are addicted to trying to inject their age away. Botox for the forehead, Collagen for the lips, Juvederm for the wrinkles around the eyes. Sometimes Beverly Hills seems like Shangri-La with a Platinum Visa card.

It amazes me what the women out here will put in their faces. Everybody wants to have a face as smooth as a baby's bottom, so what you wind up with are a whole lot of forty-five-year-old babies. Some of the ladies you see shopping on Rodeo Drive have been spackled into place, their faces are like retaining walls. And what are they trying to retain? Age? Good luck, darlings.

Don't misunderstand me. I'm not crazy about aging either, especially since I'm in the public eye courtesy of television talk shows and book tours. And I am, well, over forty. There, I said it! But I don't want to turn my face into a pincushion. My solution? Make up! It worked for the Egyptians, and it's working for me. And as for my *actual* age, if anybody asks I just say I remember the Beatles but I've forgotten The Knack. That usually covers it.

I put Tamara's book aside and returned to mine. Sometimes writing is easier than reading. I'd been at it for two hours when I finally hit save on the computer and turned to Madison.

"I think I've earned a snack," I said. "There are some Little Debbie Cakes in the pantry."

"You finished the love scene?"

"Well, you finished it. And very well too. I read what you wrote this morning, before you got here."

Madison blushed. "You said I could take a crack at it yesterday. I just kind of made some notes.'

"And they were very good ones. You understood the characters and brought their scene to a fitting resolution. You have talent, Madison."

She blushed again and headed into the kitchen. Madison was a good kid and I loved helping her out. I should have been as smart as she is when I was her age, instead of running around falling out of my halter in vampire movies and marrying a rock star. But that is a whole other story. Madison came back from the kitchen holding an apple.

"Where are my Little Debbie Cakes?" I demanded.

"When you came back from the last book tour you told me you wanted to lose ten pounds."

"Well, yes. But I don't want to have to diet to do it!"

Madison held out the apple. "This is one hundred calories."

"One hundred calories I'm never going to enjoy. I've been writing all morning!"

"Do you want to look heavy when you go on *Charlie Rose*?"

"No!"

"Well then?" The apple danced before my eyes.

"I've got a better idea," I replied. "If I can't eat, I'll shop. I'm going to Barneys." Barneys is one of the best stores in Beverly Hills, and if you shop it correctly, it can help your diet. By which I mean, an apple will help you lose weight, but I have a secret: Blazers!

That's right. A good blazer, black satin, cut on a bias, roomy at the waist, hangs over the hips, does a woman a world of good. Button it up and no one can see last night's éclairs. Which frees you up until you can get to the gym, or whatever form of torture you favor. For me it's usually a month with a personal trainer who's merciless with me before I head out on the road to sell a book.

As I walked in the front door of Barneys who should I see but a fellow writer: Tamara Osmond. And if nothing else, she was the best looking first novelists in Barneys that afternoon. Her blond hair had been cut in a page boy that framed her snub-nosed face perfectly, making her look like she was still in her late twenties.

"Tamara, how are you?" Arms outstretched, I approached her and we exchanged air kisses, the Girl Scout handshake of Beverly Hills.

"Nikki! I'm so glad to see you." She flashed me a big smile. I felt instantly guilty about her book, but what could I do?

Tamara was with her best friend, Wendy Strasser. Wendy was much more your standard issue trophy wife: long blond hair extensions with bangs, anorectic body and huge boobs, courtesy of implants. In fact, Wendy's hair was so long, and her boobs were so big that her chest resembled a theatre proscenium with the curtain parting to reveal a huge military tank charging towards the audience. Wendy had poured herself into a skintight pair of True Religion jeans and a pair of Ugg boots, topped with a white James Perse T-shirt. She was "hot" if you liked that kind of look: pushing forty, dressing twenty. No blazers for her. By comparison, Tamara, in a flowing peasant skirt so retro that it looked like it came from a 70s Greenpeace fund raiser and a Bebe top, was simple and compelling. Her look seemed thrown together, even if it had taken her hours.

"Joel just mentioned you to me," said Tamara.

"Yes, we caught up with each other yesterday at the Polo Lounge."

"He told me. And I'm so…. Do you want to grab some lunch?" she asked. I could tell that we would soon be talking about her first literary effort, but there was no escape.

Within minutes we were sitting in Barney Greengrass, the lovely café located on the back terrace of the store. In keeping with her Greenpeace motif, Tamara ordered a chopped vegetable salad. With Madison not around to stop me I went for the cheeseburger and shoestring fries.

"I brought some rice cakes with me," said Wendy. "I'll just nibble on them." I wondered if she had been moonlighting as Chloe's nutritionist.

"You've been shopping?" I noticed the twin Barneys bags at their feet.

"Oh yes." Tamara held hers up. "Something new." Inside was a Chanel belt with a red leather buckle that was studded with rhinestones.

"Something new," giggled Wendy, holding up a bag with the exact same belt in it.

Our orders arrived. Tamara and I tore into our food while Wendy munched sporadically on a very sad looking rice cake. At one point I held up a French fry on my fork and wiggled it in front of her. She screamed. I *think* she was joking.

I haven't had a chance to read your book," I said to Tamara.

"It's really wonderful," chimed in Wendy.

"You've read it?"

"The book is money," said Wendy firmly. "Absolute money." Which might have sounded a bit crass, but then Wendy was married to Lev Strasser, one of the biggest agents in town. How big? Well, he handled me, or at least his agency, Zeitgeist, did. Wendy had come to Hollywood from Australia to pursue acting, but had wound up marrying Rod Stewart instead, pretty much a requirement for any blond young thing who turns up here. When that ten minutes was up, she went back to acting. And when *that* ten minutes was up she was lucky enough to become the second Mrs. Lev Strasser. The first Mrs. Strasser had prevailed in a messy divorce, moved to Santa Barbara and opened a candle shop.

"Have you shown it to Lev?" I asked, hoping to deflect the conversation away from me.

"This is not for Lev," she replied with an air of finality. "He's too square to get it." How could Wendy be so sure? And what did she have against her husband?

"I'd hate for people to think I got a publishing deal just because I'm well connected," said Tamara.

As if people out here get them any other way, I thought.

"Well, a big agent like Lev can be quite an asset. He certainly has been for me." And I'll always be grateful to Lev Strasser for that. His literary department has kept me in my house, my Bentley, and my lifestyle, thanks to foreign rights, reprint rights and, most of all, those gorgeous Lifetime movie deals.

"We were hoping you might want to show the book to Lynn," said Wendy, mustering up her first real smile of the afternoon.

There it was. Tamara wanted to get to Lynn Mosson, my editor at Bravestone Books. And why not? Lynn had edited everyone from Stephen King to Danielle Steel during her career; she probably had the best commercial sense in the book business. People begged to be handled by Lynn. I had been lucky enough to hook up with her years ago, and, as much as anyone, it was Lynn who had helped me become the real thing, a brand name author who could sell in all territories and all media. And here were these two darling Beverly Hills trophy wives figuring they could walk right through that door on my dime. Typical.

I turned to Tamara. "Joel loves the book?"

"Totally. He thinks there might even be a movie in it."

"It's so nice the way you two have been able to manage things."

"Yes," Tamara sighed. "In some ways our divorce is turning out better than our marriage."

"Ever think of... trying again?" I figured I might as well give remarriage a plug, since Joel was clearly in favor of it.

"Why would Tamara want to do that?" Wendy gave me a sharp look. "She's moved on."

"Yes, I've moved on."

"After all," Wendy continued, "a woman has her needs." There was something in her voice, along with the way she had just talked about Lev, that made me wonder what kind of shape her marriage was in. Lev, after all, was in his mid-sixties. Wendy wouldn't have been the first trophy wife to tire of geezer sex and stray off the reservation for an afternoon or two with the pool boy. Happens all the time when the husbands are away making the money.

"You really should talk to Lynn," insisted Wendy.

"Tell me about the book," I said to Tamara, feeling trapped.

"Well, it is a trophy wife novel, but I do think it's different. There's this young girl who moves to Beverly Hills to become an actress. She starts to sleep with all these married men, and then she begins to blackmail them. Their wives get wind of the scheme and they start plotting their revenge. And then someone kills her."

"Oh, it's a murder mystery."

"Or an autobiography," Wendy said. That sent them into giggles.

"It's very true to life, Nikki," Tamara continued. "You'll recognize people and situations from our lives. I mean, I changed the names, but I based my characters on people we all know."

"Who'd you base the young girl on?" I asked. I had a good idea who it might be, but I wanted to see how much Tamara was willing to reveal.

"I have experience with bitchy young women," she replied. She had to be referring to Chloe. Wendy's face seemed to darken at the remark; I guess she didn't like Joel's daughter that much either.

"It's sweet of you to volunteer to look at it," said Wendy. Volunteer! Between the two of them and Joel this was a forced march.

"When do you think we can talk?" asked Tamara.

"Well, I'll need a few days. I've been working on my own book, but I can sneak this in. Can you wait till over the weekend, say, Monday?"

"That would be great," Tamara squealed, giving me a hug that felt very genuine. "It's so sweet of you to look at my first novel."

"Well, I can't wait to read it," I said, lying through my teeth, a phrase Lynn had told me years ago I should never use. Too clichéd.

2

I started Tamara's book the next morning.

It was just as bad as I'd feared: tons of shopping, sex every twenty pages and a plot that got lost somewhere on the 405. When the phone rang I jumped for it, grateful for the interruption.

It was Lynn, my editor. "How are you, love?" Lynn wasn't British, but like a lot of people in New York publishing, she adored letting others think she might be.

"I'm fine. Things good with you?"

"Just ducky here. Spring finally showed up and I may go to Central Park and buy a hot dog to celebrate."

So why was she calling?

"Have you got a minute?"

"Lynn, I'm reading a terrible book right now. I've got a lifetime."

"Well I got the strangest gift today, and I wanted to talk to you before I responded to it."

"What was it?"

"This morning this enormous gift basket from Dean and DeLuca was delivered right to my desk. There was a twenty pound turkey the size of Rhode Island, and it was surrounded by dried fruit and squash and onions and boxes of cornmeal. I thought the Pilgrims had landed or something. And here's the weird part. The card with the basket said "Nikki mentioned you. Love, Lev and Wendy Strasser". Can you think of any reason why he and his wife would send me all this?"

That witch, she was clever all right. "No I can't Lynn." I hated lying to her, but I didn't want to go into a long explanation about Tamara and her book and Wendy's plans for it. That had clearly been Wendy's scheme, to get me to talk to Lynn about "Revenge of the Trophy Wives," but I didn't want to buy into it until I had time to think.

"I'm not sure how to respond," mused Lynn.

"Why not send them back some Indian pudding and forty dollars in wampum? That's what the Indians did the first Thanksgiving."

She whooped with laughter. "You're no help at all."

"Everything else okay?"

"Everything else is fine, love. Thank you for asking. Send me the pages when you finish up."

"Bye Lynn." I clicked off my cell phone, threw "Revenge of the Trophy Wives" on the sofa, and turned on my computer. Might as well get some of my own work done.

* * * *

I picked up the book again the next morning.

"Good or bad?" inquired Madison.

"Evil," I replied.

Madison giggled.

"But you keep on reading."

"I'm seeing Tamara Friday. I've got to be able to tell her something about it, preferably something positive. Especially after what Wendy pulled with that gift basket to Lynn."

My cell phone rang. "Hey babe."

It was the ex-husband. Travis Tyler is his name, and I know you remember him. Certainly I do; we were married for twelve years. I met Travis when I was still an actress and he was the lead singer for the 80s metal/hair band Nausea. And I'll bet you can still sing the chorus of their big MTV hit, *Your Love is Poison*: "You got me dyin'/My heart is fryin'/Your love is poison to me" (I always thought if the writing thing dried up I could make ends meet as a heavy metal lyricist.)

Travis was half American Indian, half Scottish, a combination that turned our lovemaking into something caught midway between a war dance and a Highland fling. At six two and one ninety, with deep set eyes, a shaved chest and a head full of teased black hair that looked like five pounds of licorice strings during an earthquake, he was the sexiest man I'd ever seen. My girlfriend Maria and I saw him perform with Nausea at the Universal Amphitheatre and I talked my way back stage so I could meet him. He was dating Pat Benatar at the time, but I had a foolproof way of getting him to call. It was the 80s and networking was at its height. Everywhere you went people handed you business cards with their contact information. I did them one better. When Travis asked me for my number, I reached under my skirt, pulled down my panties and handed them to him. I'd crocheted my phone number in the crotch.

That one always worked for me, and, yes, I had some wild and crazy times when I was a kid. Why not, that's what being a kid is for. Those panties got me a call the following night, and by the next week Pat Benatar was just a memory. We got married in Vegas two months later. Dee Snyder was our best man and Heather Locklear was my maid of honor.

Now, every girl should marry a rock star at least once in her life. But then every girl needs to grow up, say about the time she hits her early thirties, and move on. Otherwise you wind up like Sharon Osbourne, dyed orange hair and trolling for gigs on second rate reality shows. Travis and I stuck it out through two international tours, a new record deal and half the band going into rehab. Along the way we saw Europe and Asia, I retired from acting (no loss there, Martin Scorsese never sent a card), and we collaborated on our most important project, our son Max. But when you're "just kids' when you get married, it makes it harder to hang together when you turn into adults. Travis and I split up seven years ago. Max is a kind of wonderful glue that keeps us together at all the important times.

"Need your help with something, babe."

"And what would that be?" I purred. I still liked my ex-husband, everybody does.

"It's not so much for me. It's for Heidi." Heidi was the new Mrs. Travis Tyler, *his* trophy wife. And she was some trophy, twenty four and a former Playmate of the Year. Heidi had a body that did not stop, for anything. And she was sweet, there was no bad blood between us. But... can I say this without being catty?... let's face it: she had the I.Q. of a gummy bear.

"Heidi has some questions about nursery school," continued Travis.

"Which one was she thinking of attending?"

"Ha, ha, ha," he chuckled. "If you're so funny, how come you're not on Jimmy Kimmel?"

"Because my audience watches *The View*. Is this about Divinity?" Heidi, a sugarholic, had named her child after her favorite candy.

"Yeah. Heidi's been looking at schools for her."

"There's the Little Red School House on Highland," I said. "Remember? Max went there."

"That's the place that barred me from the premises."

"Well, darling, you arrived for the Parent/Teacher Conference wearing a loincloth and carrying a buzzsaw."

"I was coming from rehearsal! What did they expect? All the lawyers probably arrived wearing suits. Same thing for me."

"There are some good Montessori schools in West Hollywood. Why don't you have Heidi call me. I don't bite. Not yet, anyway."

"I can do that. But I wanted to talk to you about Max."

And of course, my stomach tightened. I don't care how old your child is—Max just turned nineteen—he's still your baby. They don't tell you this when you give birth, but a mother never stops worrying, it's one of the job requirements. So, in a flash, I began to consider every terrible thing that my son could have been involved in: drugs, drugs, and more drugs.

"He wants to go to Hawaii for spring break. And I told him he should speak to you."

Sweet relief. "You mean you didn't just hand him an American Express card with five thousand dollars credited to it and tell him to send a postcard when he got there?"

"Not after the whupping you gave me when I bought him the Jeep"

I always worried that Travis and his rock star life would spoil our son. Max was a sweet funny kid with his own angle on things; he could play soccer all afternoon but still spend the evening working on his own cartoon characters, all created in the anime style. I didn't understand half his work, but it was his and I was proud of it. It might lead to something bigger someday, and I didn't want to see that drowned out by all the affluence the kids are swamped with out here. You can't raise a child by handing them an Amex card and a Porsche when they turn 18. Look what it did for Paris Hilton.

"I'll give him the cash," said Travis. "I just need it to be okay with you."

"I want him to have fun. But don't you think he should start paying for his fun sometime soon?"

"Sure, babe. But where's a UCLA sophomore gonna find a couple thou to get to the Big Island?"

"So why hasn't he called me?"

"I think he's trying to play us off against each other."

"Seems like he's done a good job." We both laughed. Max was at the stage of his life where I was his Mom, but no longer his mother. He didn't need me to pack his lunch, check his homework or schedule his haircuts. I had only two uses left now, lasagna and laundry. About every third weekend, desperate for home cooking and a break from campus, my son showed up for the afternoon. I would cook him up a huge tray of my genuinely tasty lasagna—I use chopped sirloin in the meat sauce—and he would eat about half of it, stowing the other half for the week ahead at school. Meanwhile I did his laundry. Then he would disappear and I'd wait for his next sighting in three more weeks. It was working for me.

"Okay, let's give him the dough."

"You're a peach."

"But have him call me. And Heidi too. I'll give her some school suggestions."

"Done, babe."

* * * *

I finished Tamara's book the next morning. Well, not exactly finished it, let's say I flipped through it, surveying the pages as they flew by. I did read the end though, which was a big disappointment. Instead of revealing who the killer was, Tamara pulled a switcheroo and announced that Amber had committed suicide, apparently because she felt guilty for sleeping with the husbands of all the trophy wives. This had to be wishful thinking on the scale of the Grand Canyon.

Knowing I had to do this, I called her and we made a date for lunch the next day at her house. Come morning I did some writing, some exercise, and then jumped into the Bentley. I was winding up Beverly Drive to where the houses get very large and the driveways get very long when my cell phone rang. The caller ID said Max so I picked it up, illegal here in California, but when your kid calls, your kid calls.

"Yes my love"

"So, how are you Mom?"

"You called to ask me how I am?"

"Always."

"I'm fine. How are you?"

"I'm cool."

"Well that's good. What else is new?"

"Nothing much. I'm just chilling out, hanging with some of my buds."

"Sounds like fun."

"And they're all talking about spring break, but I'm like, you know, who cares about that, it's like so much money and a big hassle."

"Uh huh." He was fishing, but I wasn't ready to let him off the hook yet.

"I mean, I suppose I could go somewhere with them if it isn't really lame or something. You know?"

"Tell me, Max, have you ever considered abandoning irony for the pleasures of real life?" For the money we both paid to put him through school, he should have had a better come on.

"What?"

"If you want to ask me something, ask me something."

"Can I go to Hawaii over spring break?"

"You're nineteen, Max. You can do what you want. We established that when you left for college."

"Well, there's, like, this little matter of the money involved."

"Ah, the money." Finally, the heart of the matter.

"I don't suppose you'd be up to lend me any?"

Why play games? He was my kid, I loved him, and I wanted him to have fun on spring break. "You don't have to worry about hitting me up, Max. Your father has already promised to bankroll you."

"That's awesome!"

"Of course it's awesome. Be sure you call him and thank him."

"I will, right now."

"And Max?"

"Yeah?"

"Do I get to see you before you leave?"

"Probably this weekend. That cool?"

"Cool, very cool.

"And Mom?"

"Yes, Max?"

"Got any lasagna?"

"Always."

"I love you, Mom."

He hung up before I got to tell him I loved him back, but that's what being 19 is about.

I switched off my phone, happy that Max was happy, and swung into Tamara's driveway. Her gray Mercedes was the only car in the driveway, so Joel and Chloe were apparently not at home. I raised the brass knocker on the front door and banged it three times. No answer. So I tried the knob and opened the door.

"Tamara? It's Nikki." Still no answer, but I wasn't convinced that Tamara wasn't there. Aside from her car in the driveway, she was simply too wound up about the book to blow me off this way. I headed down the front hallway to the kitchen.

"Tamara, are you there?"

She was. Sort of. She was dead, but she was there in the kitchen.

3

When I first saw Tamara, sprawled on the kitchen floor, a big, swollen wound on the side of her head, blood pooling around and coating her blond pageboy, I went numb. After the police arrived and it began to sink in that this was irrevocable, that she was dead, never coming back, no more lunches, no more novels, the numbness was replaced by a wave of nausea. So I appreciated it when Detective Rocco Stefano found a bottle of water for me. We were sitting in the hallway and I was answering his questions while his partners and the medical examiner were in the kitchen.

"Notice anything out of the ordinary when you came in the house?" he asked me.

"No, not really. The front door wasn't locked, but that's not strange around here when someone is in the house."

"Who was that?" he said looking up from his note pad. "Who was in the house?"

"Tamara," I said, and then I got it. "I mean she was in it, until she…"

"Until she died?"

I couldn't answer that, so the good Detective flipped the page of his note pad and started on a different tack. "Do you know of anyone who might have wanted to hurt Mrs. Osmond?"

Hurt Tamara? Funny, cheerful Tamara who used to say that there must be a God because who else would have been smart enough to create Rodeo Drive?

"Tamara wasn't the kind of person who had a lot of enemies."

"When was the last time you saw her?"

"Tuesday afternoon, I bumped into her shopping at Barneys."

"Did she say or do anything that might have indicated she was having problems?" No problems, I thought, but there was "Revenge of the Trophy Wives." I couldn't stop thinking about how Tamara had her heroine commit suicide at the end of the book. Could this be the same awful thing?

"No, it was just an ordinary day, shopping, lunch." I thought of mentioning the book, but decided against it. Why go looking for trouble?

"Was Mrs. Osmond with anyone when you saw her at Barneys?"

"Yes, she was with her friend, Wendy Strasser."

"Do you know Miss Strasser?"

"Well, yes, I do. She's actually Mrs. Strasser, the wife of Lev Strasser, the agent. His agency handles me."

The Detective was not impressed. He was all business, dressed in an unremarkable suit with a dull grey tie, right out of one of those police procedurals the networks run so faithfully. "Mrs. Strasser say anything that indicated a problem of any sort with Mrs. Osmond?"

"No, not at all."

"Can you tell me how to get in touch with Mrs. Strasser?"

"I'm sure her number is on Tamara's cell phone."

"Thank you." He flipped his notepad shut. "Would you like to step outside and get some air?"

That was the first really nice thing he'd said to me. "Sure," I replied, standing up and walking through the front door with him. As we did, I noticed that the Detective was as tall as my ex-husband Tyler. Darker features though and a huskier build. Lots of time at gym, I thought. Thinking about him helped keep my mind away from the terrible scene in the kitchen.

We stood on the slate steps where I could see two squad cars that were parked in the driveway along with an ambulance. I took another swig of water and screwed my courage up to ask the question I wanted the answer to.

"Detective, do you think Tamara could have killed herself?"

"What makes you say that?" His tone made me feel odd. "I thought you told me your friend had no problems."

I didn't want to mention the book, not yet. "You never know," I offered. "People can be on anti-depressants, bi polar…"

"Your friend didn't commit suicide, Mrs. Tyler."

"How can you be sure?"

"She died from a gunshot wound to the head. If she had killed herself, the gun would have been at her feet."

"And there's no gun?"

"Not yet."

"Could it have been a robbery, a break in?"

"Anything's possible. But nothing is missing so far. You seem to be shaken up by all this."

"Well of course I am!" I found myself exclaiming. "Someone I know has been killed. And I discovered her corpse. That doesn't happen every day, not in my daily planner."

"Did you call anyone beside us when you discovered the body?"

"No, just you… and…"

"And?" He couldn't stop pushing; after all, it was his job.

"I thought of calling Joel, her husband, but I didn't know how to…"

For the first time, Detective Stefano gave me the slightest semblance of a smile. "That's okay," he said softly. "We contacted Mr. Osmond ourselves. He was playing golf. He should be here shortly."

"I had no idea what to say to him," I confessed.

"Of course," he replied. "Like you said, this doesn't happen to you every day." Detective Stefano looked straight at me. "I think I recognize your name." God, his eyes were blue. And he had one of those Roman noses, the kind you see on ancient coins.

"That's possible."

"Are you an actress?"

"Oh no, not for years. I'm a writer, Nikki Tyler, my books are everywhere. At least I like to think they are."

"That's right. I knew I recognized the name. My girlfriend used to read your stuff. You write about Hollywood, celebrities, that kind of stuff."

"Yes, that kind of stuff." I stared up at him. The sun was behind him, and the nimbus it made around his head and torso made me think of a Greek god. Either that, or I was completely woozy from what I had just seen in Tamara's kitchen. "I can get you one of my books if you'd like."

"Afraid I don't have that much time to read. We work four day shifts straight through, ten hours a day."

"And the rest of the week?"

"Usually I grab my bike and go racing in the desert. I've got a real beauty, a classic Harley. Bought her last year." Like most men, if something was between his legs, a horse, a motorcycle, whatever, Detective Stefano referred to that something as a her. Guys, you've gotta love 'em.

"I'd like to go over your statement again, if we could," he said. So we sat on the steps of the house and reviewed what I had told him just ten minutes ago, how I had come into the house, where I found Tamara (next to the refrigerator), what I did next (screamed), and what I did after that (called the police). Detective Stefano scanned what he had written down the first time as I spoke. The pencil he held was dwarfed by his hands, big thick hands that I imagined wrapped around the handles of his classic Harley.

As he raced it in the desert sun. Probably bare-chested.

I'm totally sick, I thought to myself. I'm getting turned on to a guy at a murder scene. What's worse, he's about ten years younger than me and he has a girlfriend

"I need you to come back inside and make a positive identification," he said. "It's for official reasons."

When we got to the kitchen, the medical examiner, a young Asian woman with her hair pulled back into a ponytail, was kneeling next to Tamara and talking into a portable recorder. "Victim is five two, estimated one hundred and fifteen pounds, short blond hair, blue eyes. She had been identified as…" She turned to me. I was purposely looking away. I just didn't want to see Tamara again, not this way.

"Tamara Osmond."

She repeated the name. "Age?"

Wasn't that the big one out here? "I'm not sure, around thirty-five."

"Estimated thirty-five years old. There is a large surface wound to the right side of the head just above the ear, one and a quarter inches in diameter, with evidence of a bullet lodged in the victim's skull. Death appears to have been instantaneous."

I looked around the kitchen, still avoiding Tamara, to the counter. There was a Cuisinart, a Mr. Coffee and a white cardboard box from Sprinkles, the cupcake place on Little Santa Monica that everybody likes so much. Nothing out of the ordinary, just like I had told the Detective.

The lady examiner kept on efficiently. "Victim is wearing a blue top and a brown skirt secured by a belt. There is one earring in her left ear."

I recognized the skirt, it was the Greenpeace special Tamara had been wearing when I met her the other day. And the belt was the one she had bought at Barneys. Like the kitchen counter, nothing out of the ordinary. Except… the whole outfit just didn't work. It wasn't the kind of thing Tamara would normally let herself be seen in.

The Detective broke my train of thought. "Where can we reach you if we need to talk further, Mrs. Tyler?"

I looked around at him and his two partners, both Latinos, both very stern faced, a matching pair of intimidating cops. Could they actually think I had something to do with this?

I handed him one of my cards. "All my information is here. Is there something else I can tell you?"

"You never know." He offered me up his first big smile of the day. But it was an enigmatic one, like the kind Joel gave you when he wanted something from you. I didn't trust it. "We might have to call you to the station to make another statement."

"Would I need a lawyer for that?" I gulped. Now he had really thrown me off my game. So what if he was two hundred pounds of raw male in the early Tom Selleck mold?

"Not if you haven't done anything wrong," he said.

Okay, I said to myself, *that tears it. Let's get out of here now.* "Thank you, Detective," I said as I grabbed my bag and headed for the door. But there was a little surprise waiting for me as I got to my car, which I had reparked on the street to make room for the police cars. A news crew from KCLM, our absolutely cheesiest local station, was in the street. I saw a big blond mane of hair and an endless row of Chiclet white teeth that could only be one person, Lisa Manning, a local news reporter who made Perez Hilton look like Woodward and Bernstein. Alas, she knew me from covering benefits and red carpet events. I slapped on my Ray Bans and headed into the fray, determined to get to my car as quickly as possible.

"Nikki, can you tell me anything about this terrible tragedy?" asked Lisa sticking the mike in my face like a gun.

"It's a terrible tragedy,' I said back to her, fumbling for my keys.

"Are you involved in any way?" That was really below the belt. I opened the car door and got in.

Lisa poked her mike through the window. "Can you tell us, are there any suspects?"

"Yes," I replied, jamming my foot on the gas. "They're looking for a local news reporter. One with a bad dye job."

I sped off, leaving Lisa behind me. I spotted another news van coming up the hill. Clearly, Tamara's murder was going to be big news. And somehow, I was in the middle of it.

How I got there, I wasn't certain. That's why I wanted to go home and read her book again.

And there was one other thing: the earring Tamara had been wearing. It was the golden hoop earring with the brass monkey that I had seen her stepdaughter Chloe wearing four days earlier at the Polo Lounge.

4

That night I sat up in bed and reread Tamara's book the way she would have wanted me to read it the first time, carefully, noting every little flourish and curlicue along the way. I followed her breathless heroine, Amber, from Santa Monica to Mulholland Drive and then to the Getty Museum, where she betrayed one of her married lovers by having a quickie with a security guard in the Medieval Tapestry Gallery. I puzzled over who Amber might be and if her identity, in an unpublished manuscript, could actually be a motive for murder. It seemed a stretch.

I had just turned the page to see what mischief Amber might be up to in the Santa Barbara Mountains—a forest ranger, a new potential partner had just appeared—when I saw a handwritten notation at the top of the page. It read, "Warren Leuup, 1350 Ave. of the Stars." And that mystified me more than anything I read in Tamara's book.

Warren Leuup was one of the biggest divorce attorneys in Beverly Hills, specializing in celebrity splits. He was always retained by the husband, conniving, scheming, and, hey, sometimes even working to discredit the wife and thereby cut down her share of the pie. Tamara and Joel had split fairly amicably, and they hadn't employed Leuup to help them do it. Why then, would she have his name and address scribbled on a page of her manuscript? Did she need to ask him a research question? Had he, after all, been involved in some secret way in their divorce?

I couldn't figure that one out, so I went back to the book. By midnight, fatigue and the awful events of the day got the better of me and I dozed off.

That came to a sudden end at 6:45 the next morning when the phone rang. I bolted upright and reached for the receiver.

"Nikki!" It was a voice I knew better than any other: my mother's. She was retired and lived in Palm Springs with my father. This was not early for her.

"Did I wake you?"

"Of course you did. How are you?"

"Well you should be up, Nikki. Dad and I have already been for our walk. I've just finished my yogurt."

Mother was proud of the shape she was able to keep herself in, but that was no surprise considering that she was a former Playboy Bunny. At seventy-four, she still looked good in a bathing suit.

"How's Dad?" I asked.

"Oh he's fine. Didn't want his Metamucil this morning, but I outsmarted him. Gave him a prune Danish instead. Same result." Dad was a former stunt man, in fact, he had been Burt Reynolds' stunt double in the seventies. My folks were friendly with Burt back then, and he gave me a very big thrill when he turned up for my Sweet Sixteen party. He's a total sweetheart of a man, and I just wish he hadn't gone in for all that silly plastic surgery. What's wrong with looking human?

"I have to watch your dad," mother continued. "The women at the swimming pool keep checking him out." Dad, bless his heart, still worked out every day and had a full head of hair. "Let it go gray, just don't let it go away," was his motto.

"I'm glad to hear you're both doing well," I said.

"Us?" wailed my mother. "Nikki, it's you we're worried about. You're all over the TV."

"Good God, no. You're kidding."

"This woman with all this blond hair on the news this morning said you were seen leaving the scene of a murder! She had video of you getting into your car. And at the end she said while there are no suspects yet, several of your books have murders in them!"

Damn that Lisa Manning, anything for a story.

"Mom, I'm not a murderer."

"Well of course you're not, but I hate to see you being dragged through the mud like this."

I thought of dragging Lisa through the mud, literally. I wondered if her dyed blond roots could stand the pressure.

"Just ignore the TV, Mom. Don't watch it."

"But what happened? Are you all right?"

How do you tell your mother she shouldn't worry that you've become involved in what looks like a murder case? You don't. So I spent a few minutes calming her down and then headed to the kitchen for some coffee. I was halfway through my first cup of Costa Rican French Roast Decaf when the phone rang again.

"Good morning, love. You're up early." It was Lynn.

"My mother just called from Palm Springs. Apparently I'm on the television there."

"There too? Love, that's why I called. You've been all over the morning telly here as well."

"In New York!" I couldn't believe a story like this would go national, at least not this quickly.

"You were a hot topic on *The View*. Andrew just came in and told me." Andrew was Lynn's assistant. I always went to him for advice when I had to write a gay male love scene for one of my books.

"What would those ladies want with me?" I wailed. I usually did *The View* when I went on a book tour, and I always had a wonderful time. Like everyone, I'm awestruck by Barbara Walters's combination of Bergdorf chic and chicken soup. She's the Jewish mother we all wanted to have.

"They had footage of you leaving the murder scene, apparently. A reporter was trying to talk to you."

"Oh Lynn, calling Lisa Manning a reporter is like calling Jessica Simpson a singer."

"Whatever the venue, it still counts as '*la publicite*,'" Lynn cooed. "Andrew also told me that all your books have spiked on Amazon this morning. *The Girl from Oz* jumped fifty places back into the Top Ten!"

The Girl from Oz was my latest book, published half a year ago. It told the story of a lovely young Australian actress who must deal with a superstar marriage and cult religion before she finds happiness in the arms of a country singer who is fresh out of rehab. Some people said the book made them think of Nicole Kidman, but like all my books, *The Girl from Oz* came from the very deepest part of my creative imagination.

"Well, thanks for the sales report," I managed. "At least the public hasn't abandoned me."

"You're all right, aren't you love?" asked Lynn.

"Oh I'm fine. Just beginning to understand how O.J. Simpson may have felt the morning after."

Lynn laughed and we hung up. There were other calls, a steady stream, until I turned my cell phone off and took the receiver off my land line. Before I did, however, I knew there was one person I had to call: Joel. I'd tried the night before, but that, understandably, had been his time to turn off his phone.

It was a hard call for both of us. That was natural since Tamara had touched both our lives. But for Joel it went beyond that. He ran the gamut just like one of his pictures: sorrow, anger, despair, and even laughter. But the one thing I'll remember was how he ended the call.

Nikki, I don't know who did this, but I believe that the police will find him."

"That's what they're there for, Joel," I said.

"And when they do," he continued, "I'll kill him with my bare hands."

I worried about Joel and his vengeful state. Kill him with your bare hands? Twenty plus years of producing action movies can do bad things to you.

"Joel, you need to rest."

"I'll do that after the funeral."

"When is it?"

"Friday at the Church of the Good Shepard."

"I'll see you there. And Joel…"

"Yes?"

"I love you."

"Thanks, Nikki."

I took my second cup of coffee over to the computer and scrolled back into *Malibu Bad Boy*. Maybe doing some work would take my mind off everything.

Two hours later I was struggling with what should have been a very simple sentence. I started with "Her luscious breasts pushed against the Juicy Couture halter with the force of two cantaloupes that had been raised on steroids." That became "Her large, swelling breasts bobbled underneath the True Religion tank top like a pair of volleyballs caught in a 7.6 earthquake." I was working on "Like twin eggplants nestling on a Tuscan hilltop…" when Madison quietly came up behind me.

She surveyed my handiwork. "Nikki," she said, placing her hands on my hunched shoulders and massaging them, "you need to go to the Polo Lounge."

That is what great assistants do; they put you back in touch with yourself when you most need it. Fifteen minutes later I was being led past Henry Kissinger, Tom Ford and Starr Jones (*not* together) to the terrace of the Polo Lounge.

And while earlier this week I'd seen Joel Osmond there, today I saw someone I know almost as well, his first wife, Beverly Osmond. She was seated at a center table with Rita Collins, whose marriage to action star Palmer Collins has ended in a very messy divorce last year when he took up with a starlet. Beverly was in a Chanel suit and pearls, with her hair swept up in that kind of Iron Lady bouffant that women of a certain age favor. It makes them look as if they travel everywhere with their hairdresser in tow, a true show of power. Rita, a bit younger than Beverly, was still going for that aging gamine look, with the eggshell cut that

Shirley MacLaine made popular half a century ago. Beverly looked up, saw me and waved me over. That was it, no words, just a wave. Like I said, true power.

I walked over to the table. "Hi folks."

"We just finished," said Beverly, "but we'd love to have you join us for a bit."

As I sat down, Javier came right up to my side. "So nice to see you again."

"You too, Javier," I replied. "I'll have the McCarthy salad, dressing on the side."

"Ah yes. And to drink?"

I took a look at Beverly and Rita, two older women who had been dumped by their husbands for younger women.

"I'll have a martini."

"I didn't know you drank." Rita had gone through AA with Palmer when he had a problem back in the late nineties.

"Only when I'm awake," I said with what I hoped was a twinkle. Despite everything that had happened, I was determined to keep this a light lunch.

"How is Joel doing?" I asked Beverly.

"As well as can be expected," she replied. "I went over to the house last night, Chloe and I kept him company."

"He's lucky to have you."

"Well, yes," said Beverly, with a tiny, tight smile. "I've always thought that."

Beverly and Joel had met four decades ago at Brooklyn College where they had both been drama majors. She had actually been one of the gypsies in *Pippin* on Broadway, but gave it all up to move to Los Angeles when Joel, who had been a magician, got hired as a writer on *All in the Family*. That was the start of a very successful partnership; Joel got into producing, began making lots of money, and Beverly stayed at home, raised Chloe, and decorated the bigger and bigger houses they kept buying. Of course there were rumors about Joel playing around—a producer on location is the ultimate kid in a candy store—but Beverly seemed to be able to ignore that. Until Tamara had come along.

"I heard you found Tamara's body," said Rita.

"We were supposed to have lunch. I walked into the kitchen and there she was."

"How awful," she said with a small shudder. "Does anyone know who could have done it?"

"The police didn't have any ideas, at least not when I was there."

"They spoke to me this morning," said Beverly. "And then to Chloe. Chloe was having coffee with friends yesterday morning. And I slept in. I didn't even leave my house until one PM. We're both in the clear."

Beverly said this with the kind of finality that forbade any further discussion. "We're in the clear." Next topic. Somewhere in the distance I heard two gunshots as first Beverly, then Chloe, shot Tamara in her kitchen. Well, maybe.

"Has anyone talked to Wendy Strasser?" I asked.

"No," volunteered Rita, "I haven't heard a word from her."

"That's odd. She and Tamara were such good friends. I just ran into them this week at Barney's. Wendy was so close to Tamara."

"Well," said Beverly coolly, "I guess somebody had to be close to her."

Beverly's hatred for Tamara was pretty well known, but I was surprised to hear her airing it in the wake of her death. *Let it pass,* I thought to myself.

"Joel wasn't all that close to her any longer," continued Beverly. "The sell by date stamped on her ass was coming due any day now." *Where* was my martini?

"Oh gosh," stammered Rita, "this is all so complicated. It'd be great if we could just all be friends."

Rita was much meeker than Beverly, but when you partner with a macho movie star there's only room for one ego in the marriage. She and Palmer Collins had followed the same pattern Joel and Beverly had, meeting as struggling actors, with Rita retiring to the mansion when Palmer's career took off. He had been spotted on one of those silly Aaron Spelling shows in the 80s, *Malibu Rabbi*, and was taken under the wing of a William Morris agent who felt that the world needed a new John Wayne. What they got was a hotshot Irish boxer who loved to drink, chase women and shoot his mouth off. After kicking the booze, Palmer got religion big time, dropping his Catholicism for a feverish brand of born again Christianity. He became so involved in his new faith that he spent twenty million dollars of his own money to make a film about the birth of Christ, "Thunder over Bethlehem." Numbingly literal and graphic, the film had a thirty minute natural childbirth scene with the poor amateur actress chosen to play Mary grunting and groaning through delivery while lightning, hail and a full blown tornado crackled through the Bethlehem sky. I thought the movie was absurd, but it made over 500 million dollars worldwide, so what do I know? Palmer promptly divorced Rita and took up with the actress playing Mary, who was, presumably, no virgin.

"Here you are." It was Javier with my martini, bless him. And a bread basket, bless him twice.

"Do you mind?" asked Beverly, gesturing towards the basket.

"Not at all," I said, taking a nice, long sip on my drink, the kind that can get you through a lunch like this.

"I'm still a little hungry." Beverly picked up a poor, innocent dinner roll and dug her blood red fingernail into it. She scooped up a wad of the warm, yeasty dough and popped it in her mouth. They hadn't taken the Brooklyn out of this girl yet. Still, it was nice to see someone in Beverly Hills who still believed in eating.

"I saw you on *The View* this morning," said Rita, who, along with everybody else I knew, was apparently glued to the tube 24/7.

"You know what Gore Vidal used to say. Never turn down an opportunity to be on television or have sex."

"When was the last time you had sex?" asked Beverly.

"Oh, I don't know," I shrugged. "Probably about the same time you were on television."

"I was supposed to be on the first season of "American Idol," but they dropped me because I wouldn't screw Ryan Seacrest," Rita smirked as she slipped on a pair of Gucci sunglasses. Rita was tough, but she funny, which was what I'd always liked about her. When they were together, she and Joel were very old neighborhood.

Javier placed my McCarthy salad in front of me, another lovely pyramid of lettuce, veggies and chicken.

"Everybody orders the McCarthy here," said Beverly. "It's what the hot dog used to be to Nathan's." Now Beverly's Brooklyn roots were really showing.

"I don't," said Rita. "I've been trying to go vegetarian now that I'm… single."

"Don't you miss the meat?" I speared a forkful of my salad and tried to ignore Rita's bid for sympathy.

"Not really," she replied. "I got a cookbook last month and I've been trying out all these recipes. Legume casserole, tofu and string bean pate. They're really interesting to make. I've been spending hours in the kitchen."

"I'm afraid I've always thought that vegetarian cooking was like lesbian lovemaking," I said. "A whole lot of work for not a lot of return." I shoveled another forkful of the delicious McCarthy into my mouth.

Beverly laughed. "Well you're not a cook, Nikki. You never have been. You're a writer."

"Scribble, scribble," I nodded as I kept on with my salad.

"You could become a cook though," said Rita, ever the optimist. "I mean you could take some cooking classes and then you could use the recipes in your books."

"Why would I want to do that?"

"Oh, lots of authors are doing it," Rita continued. "I just finished a book that had the best recipe for brownies in it. Vegan brownies, no eggs."

"Oh Rita," I replied, "those are those cozy little mysteries they write for the ladies who enjoy dreaming of food while they read. That's not my thing."

"No?" she replied.

I shook my head as I polished off the last of the McCarthy salad. "Those sweet little books are food porn. I'm into... the real porn! I'm selling scandal, not scallops."

"That's why you sell so well, darling," said Beverly, patting my hand reassuringly. "People may cut down on their food, but they always want their sex."

"Besides," I said, "most of those authors throw in a recipe because they don't know how to end the chapter."

NIKKI TYLER'S MARTINI SCALLOPS

1 lb. scallops
2 tbsp. olive oil
2 tbsp. butter
Salt
Pepper
One large pitcher of Martinis

Mix up one strong pitcher of vodka martinis, serve in chilled glasses and sip constantly while cooking.

Melt butter in frying pan, mix in olive oil. Toss in scallops, sauté two minutes each side. Add salt and pepper to taste.

Drain butter and oil from pan. Pour approximately one martini from the pitcher into frying pan. Stir lightly while liquid reduces.

Serve scallops on mushroom risotto. Or Rice-A-Roni. If the martinis are good enough, you'll never notice the difference.

Serves four.

5

Robertson Boulevard between Beverly and Third is the place to shop in Beverly Hills if you're under thirty. It's Rodeo Drive for the Facebook set, and an afternoon spent there can make you feel like you're trapped in a music video. But after I had finished my lunch at the Polo Lounge with Beverly and Rita Collins, I knew I had to go there. Robertson was where Chlothes, Chloe's boutique, was located.

On my way I over, I called Wendy Strasser on my cell phone. Illegal again, but this was about a murder and I hadn't spoken to her since I had discovered Tamara's body.

No luck, my call went into her voice mail.

I found a space right on Robertson, parked my car, and fed the meter a fistful of quarters. Parking now costs two dollars an hour in Beverly Hills; soon I'm sure the city will be selling spaces on the street as cardominiums. They'll probably sell out.

I walked past storefront after storefront filled with distressed jeans that cost upwards of five hundred dollars, and edgy little tops in mango, vermillion, and hot pink. Not a drop of navy blue anywhere. It's great to dress like a clown when you're a kid.

Midway down the block I came to the Ivy, the restaurant that's famous for its crabcakes and its movie stars. It has a lovely outdoor patio with a white picket fence around it: set dressing to make you feel you've stumbled upon a sweet little down home dive in the midst of trendy Beverly Hills. Which you have, provided the down home dive you grew up eating at served crabcakes for twenty-four dollars a pop.

There was a small mob of photographers around the Ivy; they hang there all afternoon to try and get photographs of the movie stars who come for the food, all of it delicious. If you want to see Richard Gere slurping down corn chowder, this is the place to go to.

I had just made it past the entrance when a huge black Escalade rumbled up to the valet parking station at the curb. Behind the tinted windows of the vehicle you could hear a rap lyric booming from the sound system, "You my ho/I want some mo!"

From the depths of this 3,000 pound chrome and steel monster, to the accompaniment of the above love lyric, emerged a 98 pound waif in blond pig tails. She was wearing a huge pair of Chanel sunglasses and carrying a tiny shiatsu in her right hand. The paparazzi pounced on her, snapping what seemed like hundreds of pictures in the 30 seconds it took her to get out of the passenger seat. Laci Stivers had arrived at the Ivy.

For several years now she'd been famous as *the* Hollywood party girl, queen of the clubs and darling of the tabloids. She was the heiress to the Stivers real estate fortune—Daddy built shopping malls all over the country with Chinese co-financing. Laci was a celebrity even though she didn't do anything. Well she did do one thing, publicity. As the old joke went, she would go to the opening of an envelope in order to get her name in the papers. And it had worked for her; she'd become Andy Warhol famous, but for way more than fifteen minutes. She'd parlayed the fame into a silly reality TV show, *I Love Laci*, and a clothing line produced by slave labor in Ecuador, advertised in *Vanity Fair* and sold at Target. Like so many other MTV maidens, Laci was famous for breathing; an "it' girl for a society that had forgotten what "it" was.

Bounding out of the driver's seat to join her at the curb was a tall, olive skinned man of about thirty with thick black hair . He had the kind of body you see on those infomercials for abs machines, ninety nine percent lean muscle, one percent fat. He was very Hollywood casual, a two day growth of stubble, a Dodgers baseball cap and an Ed Hardy T-shirt that was practically wallpapered over his nipples. He slung his arm over Laci's shoulder in a very familiar manner. The two of them posed for the cameras, and the sounds of the shutters almost drowned out the rap song that still boomed from the Escalade, now handed over to a valet parker.

"Laci, over here!" shouted one of the paparazzi.

She turned towards him, Mr. Gorgeous on her right, the poor shiatsu suspended between them, an animal sacrifice on the altar of fame. The terrified little dog began to bark.

"Be patient Coco!" trilled her owner. "Laci's almost finished." Like some monarchs, Laci had apparently taken to referring to herself in the third person.

"Give them a few more." Her escort turned her towards yet another group of eager photographers. He flashed a big smile, the kind you flash after you've spent thousands on porcelain veneers for your teeth.

Then he and Laci walked up to the terrace of the Ivy and sat at a table with Vance Packer. Good Lord, I thought to myself, the boy band rides again.

Vance had been the lead singer of Playerz, a ridiculously popular boy band in the late nineties. When the group broke up, he went into a brief eclipse, only to reemerge as the founder of a new "religion" which he called Luna. It would be more accurate to say he called it Luna and he called it a religion. Because Vance's idea was nothing more than a self-help philosophy, one part Dr. Phil, one part Norman Vincent Peale, dressed up in some spiritual double speak. There was no God or higher being involved with Luna, only a self-referential, deeply narcissistic outlook that encouraged people to rationalize their shortcomings while "getting ahead in life." One of Luna's mantras, posted on billboards all over Southern California, was "Wealth is God's Way of Telling You He Loves You." With a saying like that, Luna had become very popular, very quickly in Beverly Hills. Palmer Collins, Rita's ex, was a recent convert to Luna. And now, it appeared, so was Laci.

"I'm feeling very spiritual," squealed Laci to Vance, handing him her tiny, trembling dog. Mr. Gorgeous looked on impassively.

"Great," said Vance. "Let's have cheeseburgers and meditate on that." His looks had gone a little puffy, but he still had that all American boy band smile.

I'd seen enough people lose money to Scientology to know a scam when I saw one, so I turned away quickly, only to bump into a heavyset photographer with no less than four cameras slung around his neck. He had an enormous Rolex on his wrist and a tangle of wiry hairs peeked out of his open white dress shirt like a thousand tiny snakes.

"Aren't you Nikki Tyler?" he boomed.

"Oh no," I said, quickly slipping on my sunglasses. "She's in rehab."

"Well, aren't you somebody?" he persisted.

I'm nobody," I replied. "Who are you? Are you nobody too?" Not believing that I had just managed to quote my favorite poet, Emily Dickinson, to a Hollywood paparazzi, I walked away at a fast clip, passing Kitson, the store that anchored Robertson, and on to the doorway of Chlothes.

Looking up at the windows, I had to admit they were very clever. There were two mannequins in each window, two men in one, two women in the other. The mannequins were holding hands and had been posed in wedding tableaux, the men in tuxes, the women in bridal gowns. But their heads had been removed, replaced by cantaloupes. And in each window was a sign that read "Can't Elope," a clear reference to the fact that gay people still couldn't get married in California. Some skillful West Hollywood window dresser had been working overtime.

I walked into the store, which was stocked with the same types of jeans and tops that every other store on Robertson was showing. Three young Japanese women, all with iPods plugged in their ears, were examining a yellow vinyl miniskirt with huge black zippers on both sides. Otherwise the place was dead.

Approaching a young saleswoman with purple eye shadow who was reading *The Secret*, I said, "Excuse me, is Chloe here?"

She looked up from her book, barely disguising the utter boredom my question had triggered. "Is she expecting you?"

"I'm an old family friend," I continued, feeling like someone out of Dickens calling on a rich relative. "My name is Nikki Tyler."

"I'll see if she's free." The girl walked to the back of the store.

It was almost five minutes before she returned, and it occurred to me that the Japanese girls could have picked the place clean had they wanted to. But they kept bobbing their heads to their iPods, picking through one skirt after the next. Finally Chloe emerged from the back of the shop, a Pinkberry yogurt cup in her hand.

"Hello, Nikki,' she said, sounding uncertain.

"I just had lunch with your mother. She told me your father is okay, and I wanted to make certain that you are."

Chloe turned to the salesgirl. "Why don't you go help them?" She gestured towards the Japanese girls.

With her hired help out of ear shot, Chloe turned back to me. "I'm fine, thank you. It's nice of you to ask." She spooned some of the yogurt into her mouth.

"I just can't help feeling that we're all in this together. It happened in your house, I discovered Tamara, and…"

"Yes," Chloe said, cutting me off. "But everything is being handled. Daddy's, well, he's as good as can be expected. And Mom is fine. And I spoke with the police this morning. I'm in the clear."

In the clear. That seemed to be the lucky phrase for the day.

"I wasn't sure you'd be here." I said.

"Where else would I be?" she replied. "It's not as if my life is over."

There was an awkward silence; Chloe seemed to realize how inappropriate that last remark had been.

"Lookit, Nikki," she said, "I'm upset for Daddy because he loved Tamara. And anything that hurts him, hurts me. He was there for me when I had to kick drugs, and I love him for that. He's my rock. So I want to give him his affirmations."

"Affirmations?"

"Dr. Phil says they're very important." Oh. "But I'm not going to pretend that I liked Tamara or anything."

"Well, you managed to live in the same house with her." I'd always thought it was crazy of Chloe to go on living in the house after Joel and Tamara had divorced.

"Where else was I supposed to go? It was my house too!"

"Chloe, lots of people move on in life. They get their own places."

"I'm trying to run a business here." She gestured with the yogurt spoon like it was a scepter. "This takes a lot of money."

"I thought your father, well, I thought he helped you out a bit."

"Is that some sort of crime?" she whined. "Like Tori Spelling got to be an actress because she's so talented and beautiful? Besides, all Daddy ever did was help with the rent here, which is a fortune, a total fortune. The rest of his money was all tied up by her."

"Tamara?"

She slipped a spoonful of yogurt in her mouth and then sucked on the spoon like a naughty little child. "You know how crazy Daddy was about her, even after they got divorced. He gave her anything she wanted."

Which, of course, was what Joel had done with Chloe too. And it hadn't worked very well. She didn't need affirmations, and closure, and Dr. Phil hugfests. She needed a good, hard spanking. I thought Joel was right to push her to make the business work and not just keep underwriting her.

"There's something else I wanted to ask you about," I said.

Chloe looked at me blankly. "What?"

"Do you remember those earrings that you were wearing when I saw you earlier this week at the Polo Lounge? The gold hoop ones with the little monkeys?"

"If you want to buy a pair, I'll have to order them. We're out of stock."

"How long would that take?"

"I don't know, probably about a week. I've got to order another pair of them for myself anyway."

"You want another pair?" I said, thinking I might be on to something.

"Damn right," said Chloe. "Someone must have stolen my first pair. I've looked everywhere for them and I can't find them." She put her Pinkberry cup and spoon down on the glass counter and left it there, as if she were in McDonald's, rather than her own upscale boutique. Amazing.

"So you lost the earrings?"

"They disappeared two days ago. I have no idea where they are. What's it to you?"

I didn't know whether to believe her or not. It made no sense that Tamara would have stolen her earrings, but then who else could have?

I couldn't pursue it any further because just then the door opened and in swept Laci Stivers. Her sunglasses were perched on her head, but she had left her shiatsu and Mr. Gorgeous back at the Ivy.

"Chloe," she whooped, "We're having cheeseburgers with Vance Packer and then we're going to a Luna meeting with him. Why don't you join us?" The two of them were girlfriends, in fact Chloe had even guest starred on "I Love Laci" a few times.

She turned abruptly from me, the old business, to Laci, the new business. "I was just entering some sales figures for the month," she said.

"Oh come on," insisted Laci, who took absolutely no notice of me. "You can do that any time. After all, there'll be another month next month." The irrefutable logic of the undereducated super-rich.

"I guess I could use a break." The Japanese girls had spotted Laci and were whispering and giggling animatedly. Used to being stared at constantly in public, she simply ignored them and looked around the store instead.

"You don't have any of my dresses for sale," she pouted.

"Laci, your dresses are at Target for fifteen dollars. I charge more for a hair scrunchie," Chloe replied. She gestured towards a small bin of multi-colored, sequin covered scrunchies. The sign on them read $25.00.

"We ordered you a cheeseburger, so you've really got to join us."

"All right." Chloe swept her Pinkberry cup and spoon into the trash basket and grabbing her purse, a Hermes Birkin crocodile number that probably cost more than she paid her salesgirl monthly.

"Nikki, I've got to run," she said, turning to me. "We can talk more later."

"Have fun," I replied. "I'll just hang out and maybe buy a scrunchie." She and Laci were out the door and the salesgirl, suddenly solicitous, was at my side.

"You'd like a scrunchie?" she asked.

"Actually, I think I'll pass. I've got some old rubber bands at home that may suit me just as well."

"Chloe told me you were a writer." The salesgirl offered a small smile, one that held the tiniest drop of condescension in it.

41

"Yes. And I can see you're a reader." I pointed towards her copy of *The Secret*.

"Actually, that's just a prop," she said. "They taught us in merchandising class that holding a book makes the customer feel you're a deep thinker."

"Well you certainly had me fooled."

6

The day's events, lunch with Beverly and Rita, Chloe, the television coverage, sufficiently exhausted me that I fell into a very deep sleep that night. I woke up rested and ready to hit the keyboard. I blazed away at *Malibu Bad Boy*, moving my once hateful hero through the joys of Judaism—chopped liver! aisle seats for "Fiddler"! – as he neared what would be his mid-life religious conversion and a tardy, but heartfelt, bar mitzvah. The writing turned out to be just the therapy I needed. Who says escapist literature has no value?

By noon I had seven pages done—you always write more as you come to the end of a book, a kind of finish line mentality takes over—and was happily showing them to Madison who had arrived for the afternoon.

"Wow." She pulled off her reading glasses. "You did all this this morning?"

"Nothing like a murder to get the creative juices flowing."

"Think that's Stephen King's secret?"

"Oh, I bet his talent and hard work have a lot do with it," I replied, thinking about Tamara and her now dashed hopes of becoming a trophy wife author. I still wondered if her book hadn't somehow been the reason she was killed.

"Nikki, I have to warn you about something." Madison put the pages back on my desk. "I was at *TMZ* this morning and they're going to be covering Tamara's murder. It's up on the board as the third most important story of the day."

I uttered a long, heartfelt "Ugh" as I sank back deeper into my chair. "What were the two more important stories?" I asked.

"Madonna's rumored plastic surgery and Pam Anderson's rumored breast reduction."

I howled in disbelief as Madison flashed an apologetic smile. "What can I say?" she added, "this is Hollywood."

"Just what I need," I moaned. "A news crew at the end of the driveway."

"According to the news desk, they're covering the Osmond house, at least for this afternoon."

"Madison, do they know you work for me?"

She looked troubled for a second, and it wasn't hard to figure out why. It's tough to be young, ambitious, and serving two masters.

"No," she said with a sigh. "I haven't told them."

"Well if you have to, I understand. As long as you don't feed them private information: a job is a job."

"God, you're the boss everyone dreams about," she said.

"Oh yeah, that's me. The Devil Wears Banana Republic. Just don't spill the coffee on my new pages."

Madison grinned and grabbed my seven pages worth of blood, sweat and tears just as the doorbell rang.

"Could you get that?" I asked. "I don't want to answer the door if there's a reporter on the other side."

"Done." She headed into the hallway.

She was back a moment later with none other than Detective Stefano.

"Mrs. Tyler, I was wondering if I might ask you a few more questions?" he said. The Detective was much more casually dressed today, a light blue tennis shirt and Dockers. It only made him look hotter, dammit.

"Okay," I replied. "Let's go into the living room."

He followed me across the hallway to what Travis and I had called the den of iniquity. A couple of big brown leather sofas faced each other, with a glass coffee table mounted on an old Fender guitar between them. I'd been meaning to redecorate for years.

"Jellybean?" I offered the Detective a candy from a large silver Tiffany bowl sitting on the coffee table. Another hangover from the rock star wife syndrome. *I'm calling a decorator tomorrow,* I said to myself.

"No thank you," he replied. "I came to see you because I thought you might be able to help me locate Wendy Strasser. You did say you saw her and Mrs. Osmond right before the crime."

"Yes, at Barneys. We had lunch."

"And you haven't heard from her since?"

"Detective, if you want to find where Wendy Strasser is, you should speak to her husband, Lev."

"I've done that," he replied evenly. "Mr. Strasser hasn't heard from his wife in two days. Apparently they hadn't been spending that much time together lately."

So that was what Wendy meant at Barneys when she said that she wasn't talking much to Lev. Another divorce? God, the town was full of them. It wasn't the first wives' club or the second wives' club, it was a revolving door. Men traded their wives in like last year's car, always looking for a sleeker model with better mileage. Well it was damn well time we women threw up a highway blockade and...

Crack! I was jolted from my interior monologue by the snap of a pistachio nut being opened.

I looked over to the Detective to see him chomping down on the nut. He reached over to the bowl on the table, a matching bowl to the one that held the jellybeans, and grabbed another pistachio.

"So you like the nuts?" I said.

"Yeah," he replied popping it in his mouth, "I like the nuts."

"But you haven't found Wendy?"

"No, but if you hear from her, or about her, I'd like you to call me." He handed me his card, then scooped up some more nuts.

"Detective, have you learned anything more about Tamara's death?"

Crack! "Were you two close?" he asked.

"Pretty close. I'm a friend of Beverly Osmond, Joel's first wife, so there was that."

"But you were going to have lunch with her."

"Yes, but that was because…" I decided it was time to come clean. "That was because Tamara had written a book. She asked for my help with it."

"And you're a big time author."

That almost made me blush. "I don't know exactly how big time…"

He traced his thumb over the two halves of the next nut's shell, inserting his nail in the tiny crevice that lay between them. *Crack!* "No, I mean it," he said. "I told you my girlfriend reads your stuff."

"She likes it, I hope."

"I don't know," he replied, "I never asked her. And now that we're split up…"

I reached over, grabbed a pistachio and opened it gleefully. So he was single! Time for a celebration. *Crack!* I gobbled down the nut.

"I mean," the Detective continued, "I've never read any of your books, but I pretty much know about them from what she told me. Movie stars, fashion, money. It's kind of a chick lit thing, right?"

I was warming to the conversation by the moment. "Actually, my stuff is a bit racier than a lot of the books written for women. I tend to have strong female characters, lots of action and lots and lots of sex."

"Oh," he smiled. "Then I might like your books after all."

"You might at that."

"And they're not chick lit?"

"I prefer to think of them as clit lit."

Crack! "I'll pick one up on the way home tonight," he said.

45

I sank back on the sofa, feeling relaxed at last. "So, Detective, can I assume from this conversation that I am not a suspect in Tamara's murder?"

"You're not a suspect," he said carefully. "At this time, you are not a suspect."

"Well that's good," I replied. "Have yourself another nut."

He leaned over, grabbed one from the bowl and... *Crack!*... opened it. "I should tell you though, Mrs. Tyler," said the Detective, "you could, at this time, be considered a person of interest."

"Oh Detective," I said with a smile, "I've always been that. All my life."

* * * *

After Detective Stefano left, I took a cold shower. Oh, I didn't *really* need it, but it's great to feel clean and fresh, and I had somewhere to go. I had decided that I had to see Lev Strasser and try to find out what happened to Wendy.

If you want to see Lev, you need only go to his office at Zeitgeist, in Century City. The agency occupies the top two floors of one of those gorgeous, soulless steel and glass skyscrapers on the Avenue of the Stars. As the founder of Zeitgeist, Lev could have saved his company almost $50.00 a square foot by taking space on the middle floors, but that was anathema to his image of running the most ruthless agency in town. He insisted on the top floors, despite the hefty price. "Better for the suicides," he told Wendy when he signed the lease.

If that last remark makes Lev sound heartless, well, let's just say that the junior agents at Zeitgeist didn't call him the Tin Man for nothing. A former business partner, who split with him before he founded the agency, once described Lev as Richard III but with a smaller hump and less charm.

Actually he has no hump and, when he wants to, considerable charm. Like many deeply driven people, Lev never stops working, and if it's not for his business, it's often for charity. He raised close to twenty million dollars for Cedars Sinai for the research and treatment of breast cancer, a disease that had killed Wendy's mother. I always loved him for that, and assumed that Wendy did too.

As for whether or not they were *in* love, who knew? At 57, short and fat, with a shaved head that he constantly mopped dry with a handkerchief because he sweated so much, Lev was far from an Adonis. I had always figured that he took care of Wendy, and that was enough to keep the home fires burning. You know the deal, just lay back and close your eyes. There were so many women doing that in Beverly Hills, I figured they had all gone for the same procedure, having a picture of George Clooney tattooed on the inside of their eyelids.

Now you can't just walk into a major agency unannounced, a fact that the young women who sit at the front desks, a Guccied Palace Guard, are well aware of. The one at Zeitgeist looked up from her computer as I announced myself.

"And you're here to see?" she inquired coolly.

"Lev Strasser."

"He's expecting you?"

"No, but I made this agency over a hundred thousand dollars last year. Perhaps he'll want to see me regardless."

A minute later one of Lev's assistants was walking me into his office. The enormous corner room was immaculate, furnished with just a large glass table, an Eammes chair, and a Julian Schnabel hanging on the far wall. There was a Blackberry and a pitcher of water on the table, nothing else. A curved glass wall at the end of the room, outfitted with a door, led to a terrace and a spectacular view of the westside of Los Angeles. But the Zen-like calm of the room was deceptive. When Lev was angry, he used more profanity than a rap star with Tourette's syndrome.

"Nikki!" He rose from the chair to shake my hand. "This is a surprise."

"Yes, I hope you don't mind."

"Not at all. My clients are my business."

There were some palm trees on the terrace and, from where I was standing, it looked as if one of them was growing out of Lev's head. On him it looked good.

"I guess I don't get a chair?" I looked around the room.

"I've been having everything redone, my chairs are due back in week. Let's go out to the terrace."

We sat on a pair of Italian outdoor chairs while his assistant brought the refreshments, mango ice tea for me, more water for Lev. I looked out over the other skyscrapers of Century City, all the way to the Santa Monica Bay.

"I love this view," I said.

"You didn't come here for the view," he replied.

"You're right. I came here because I'm caught in the middle of something, Tamara's murder."

"What a rotten business." Lev grimaced. "I spoke to Joel yesterday. God, he loved her so much. He's destroyed, just destroyed."

"How's Wendy been taking it?" I asked. "She and Tamara were so close."

"Wendy hasn't been around much lately." He said it as a matter of fact, almost as if he weren't her husband.

"Do you know where she is?"

Lev took out a handkerchief and rubbed his head. "You're just like that cop who was here the other day. You working with him?"

"No," I laughed. "I'm not a very good candidate for the police force. But I need to ask you something. Did you and Wendy send my editor a huge gift basket the other day?"

"Lynn? Why the hell would I send Lynn a gift basket?"

"Well if it wasn't you, perhaps it was Wendy. The basket was from Dean and DeLucca."

"I hate that place. They overcharge for everything, especially the salami," he groused.

"So maybe it was Wendy?" I asked.

"Who the hell knows if it was? That's her business, not mine." He dismissed the subject out of hand with a wave of his handkerchief.

I looked Lev straight in the eye, no pretense, no sentiment. *Be sincere*, I told myself. *That's something most agents have never seen.*

"Lev, has something happened to Wendy?"

He jumped out of his chair. "How the hell should I know? I haven't heard from her in two days now."

"Have you been living apart?"

"In different parts of the house. But sometimes, she disappears. I don't ask." He was rubbing his skull with the handkerchief again, this time in a circle. All he needed was a little Endust.

"You're getting a divorce then?"

He took his seat and gave me a hard look. The drama was over; the agent was back. "That's none of your goddamned business, baby." His sneer came right out of an old Harold Robbins paperback.

"Don't call me baby."

Lev reached out swiftly and took my hand. Now he was soothing, milk and honey, the other side of the agent.

"Nikki, forgive me," he said in a soft voice, the kind you use for lovemaking or closing deals. "I've known you forever. I love you. You've been like family. But my situation with Wendy, and now this awful thing with Tamara, it's all been too much for me."

"Will you tell me if you locate her, Lev?" I asked. "It might help us find out what happened to Tamara."

Lev looked out at the view, the hazy sunshine hanging over the endless blocks of condos, restaurants, laundromats, furniture stores, yogurt shops, nail salons and taco trucks that made up the westside of L.A.

"This town," he said with an undertone of disgust. "Who knows where the hell she could be in this town?"

7

Lev walked me to the elevators, past the receptionist who looked up and was suitably impressed that the head of the agency was seeing me out. Maybe next time she wouldn't be so chilly. Fat chance.

"I'll call when I hear from Wendy," he said. 'When' rather than 'if.' That was hopeful.

"Thanks, Lev." I leaned over and giving him a quick kiss on the cheek. The elevator doors opened and I stepped in.

That's when I started to get nervous. You see, I have this thing about elevators in tall buildings. Not when they go up; I'm fine with that. But going down to the lobby is always trouble for me.

There's a reason for this. When my father was a stuntman in the seventies one of the biggest films he worked was *The Towering Inferno*. Remember that one, the all-star barbecue starring Paul Newman and Steve McQueen, with all the supporting players getting flambéed throughout the film?

Dad took me to the set the day they filmed the scene where all the female stars were huddled in an outdoor elevator as it slid down the side of the building, jammed and started spilling them out onto the pavement. Faye Dunaway had to hold on for dear life (her billing saved her), but Jennifer Jones wound up as road kill in a white Galanos gown.

Courtesy of being the stunt coordinator's teenage daughter, I got to ride in the elevator when Dad and his crew took it for a test drive. We were going down the five floors they had built for the set, when suddenly the elevator slammed to a halt and, just like poor Jennifer, I spilled out onto the studio floor where, fortunately, a huge air pillow cushioned my fall. Ever since then, I've hated going down in elevators.

So I held my breath as the car descended from the 28th floor to the 15th where, not as smoothly as I might have wished, it came to a halt. Two Russian security guards got in. One of them took out a pack of cigarettes as we started descending again.

"You want a smoke?" he said to his friend.

"No. I want a bath and then I want to screw your wife."

They broke into chuckles as the car lurched onto the 9th floor and my stomach lurched along with it. A beautiful young Filipino woman, wearing a tiny yellow dress that looked like it had been a Kleenex in its former life, boarded. The two men fell silent as they inspected her like she was a new car.

I thought we might be home free, but we stopped short on seven where three bored office workers, all with iPods plugged into the ears, entered the car. I was breaking out into a sweat and fighting back nausea.

When we reached the lobby and everyone exited, I was reeling. The office workers walked right past me and the two security guards followed the Filipino woman like a pair of hunting dogs. I staggered over to one of the lobby's marble walls and pressed myself against it, letting the cool stone revive me and calm my queasy stomach.

A lobby guard approached me. "Are you all right, miss?"

"Yes, I'm fine," I croaked, as I gathered myself up. "Just took the elevator ride a bit hard. Made me feel nauseous." I slipped on my sunglasses and prepared to leave.

That's when I noticed the building directory, right next to where I had practically fainted. 1350 Avenue of the Stars. I looked over the listings. Of course! Warren Leuup had his law office here. The very same Warren Leuup whose name had been written in Tamara's manuscript.

He was on the fifth floor. That wasn't so bad. If I felt dicey about riding down again, I could always use the stairs. I headed back to the elevators.

"Miss?" It was the lobby guard.

"Yes?" I replied as I pushed the up button.

"I thought you said the elevator made you nauseous."

"It did, but I left my anti-depressants in the office." That kind of excuse always works around here. The doors opened and I slipped into the car.

Getting off on the fifth floor, I walked down the corridor to Warren Leuup's office, suite 510. I prepared myself to deal with yet another young Palace Guard, only to be met with a lovely surprise when I pulled open the huge oak door that read Leuup and Spangler, Attorneys at Law.

Sitting behind the receptionist's desk was a striking black woman, silver gray curls framing her delicately carved features. She was wearing a red wool minidress that showed off every curve of her still gorgeous figure.

"Inez!" I cried.

"Nikki Tyler." She rose to give me a hug. "I haven't seen you since Snoop Doggy Dog's wedding!"

Inez Carver had been a backup singer in Tyler's band for what had proved to be a very misguided idea, a heavy metal soul review. Tyler would kill me for saying it, but Inez had probably been the best thing on stage. Which was no surprise since she had earned her stripes back in the seventies and eighties doing backup for Boz Scaggs and Bob Seeger, among others. Inez's seductive crooning had made those middle aged rockers, my ex included, look better than they really were. Plus, she was supposed to be the great, great granddaughter of George Washington Carver, who had discovered over 500 uses for the peanut. Which was kind of funny, because Inez was the first person I ever met who had an allergy to peanuts.

"What are you doing here?" I said as she slipped back into her seat.

"Making a living like everybody else," Inez said. "Rock and roll doesn't pay the bills anymore."

"But you're such a great singer. Doesn't anybody need a really good backup woman?

"Honey," she purred, lowering her thick black eyelashes, "a lot of men might need that, but right now they're not paying a salary for it." When she was starting out, Inez had dated three of the Four Tops and four of the Jackson Five.

"Is Andre still around?" Inez had been married to Andre Jarvis, a really great saxophone player, when she had toured with Nausea.

"Oh he's around, from time to time. But we got divorced four years ago and I still have Tyrone to raise."

"Is that how you wound up here? Warren Leuup did your divorce?" Good news or bad, I was thrilled to be talking to Inez again.

"Warren Leuup!" she laughed. "With the prices they charge here? Judge Judy is more my style. No, I wound up here through a temp agency. They were looking for someone to sit up front and answer calls. The personnel lady didn't seem that thrilled with me, but Warren walked by during the interview, leaned his head in the office, and when I got home I had a message on my machine."

"He liked your style?"

"Let's say he liked my skirt," Inez said with a wink.

"Which was?" I asked as I laughed.

"Just like this one," she said as she stood up again and I saw that her dress stopped mid-thigh, showing off her gorgeous black legs.

"How do you do it?" I moaned, readjusting my beloved black Armani blazer.

"Well, I've got a fourteen year old to raise, I exercise three times a week, and I only allow myself fried chicken on Sunday nights."

It ticked me off that this great looking, talented woman had to field phone calls for a living, but there you have it.

"Now why are you here?" asked Inez. "I thought you and Tyler got divorced a long time ago."

"We did, but I wanted to see Warren Leuup about something, not a divorce. I don't suppose you could get me in to see him?"

"Of course I can," winked Inez. "I told you he liked me."

I gave her a hug. "It's so good to see you again, Inez."

"Same here, honey."

I took out my card. "Listen, everyone here says let's do lunch and nobody ever does it, but I really want to sit and talk with you. Will you call me?"

"Of course I will." She slipped the card into her purse. "Anything else I can do for you?"

"How long have you been here?"

"Six months."

"In that time, has Lev Strasser ever come in the office?"

"Mount Baldy up there?" said Inez, cocking her head upward. "Yeah, he was in here about two weeks ago."

"Divorcing?"

"You never know what it's about when the big guys come in. Sometimes it's social, charity stuff, sometimes they're shuffling the deck. But he was in here."

"Thanks, Inez. I want to do lunch soon."

She gave me a great big smile, just like she used to give the audience back in her touring days. Bubbling brown sugar with a dab of cream on top.

"Let me get Warren for you."

* * * *

"You're a friend of Inez's?" Warren Leuup said to me as he closed a folder and placed it in a very tidy out box that was counterbalanced by an equally tidy in box on the other side of his desk. Everything was just so, which had to be the way he liked things to be.

"Yes, we've known each for years."

"Inez is a character," he said. "She brings some life to our office."

"Well, of course," I said. "Inez is nothing but life. Believe me, I know. We met during a rock and roll tour."

"That must have been interesting," he said, betraying not even a speck of interest. Warren Leuup was the divorce lawyer of your nightmares, pale skin, dyed orange hair tortured forward, and thin pasty lips. He actually looked more like a vampire than a legal representative, which, if you were his client, would make him a hell of a lawyer.

"Are you a rock fan, Mr. Leuup?"

"When I was an associate back in the seventies, before I got into marital work, I defended Grace Slick on a pot charge," he replied. "Does that count?"

"Only if you inhaled." I chuckled. Not even a smile from him. Lawyers.

"I assume you're not here to discuss rock and roll, Mrs. Tyler," he said politely.

"Well, I know that you're a highly respected divorce lawyer," I replied, stalling for time and trying to work up an angle.

"And you're thinking of a divorce?" he asked.

"You never know." Another stall. I guess he didn't know about Tyler and me.

"Well, it was nice of Inez to steer you to me, but as she should know, I primarily represent men in divorce litigation. However we have some female associates here that I would be glad to introduce you to."

"I think I might be more comfortable being represented by a man."

"That's your prerogative." He folded his hands neatly in front of him as if he were going to make a confession. "But I am almost always on the husband's side; it's the way my career has evolved. Perhaps it has to do with empathy. My own divorce taught me a great deal."

I recalled now that Warren Leuup was the veteran of an ugly divorce a few years ago, with details about his wife's infidelity leaking out in the Los Angeles Times. But for whatever embarrassment it caused him, all the innuendo forced her to accept a much smaller settlement than she might have gotten otherwise. Maybe that was the blueprint for his clients' cases.

"Tamara Osmond also recommended you." I said. There had to be a reason why his name had been in the book.

"Joel Osmond's wife?" he said blandly. "The woman who was murdered the other day?"

"Yes, I was a friend of hers."

"I can't imagine how that can be, Mrs. Tyler. I never met Mrs. Osmond. Or her husband. I only knew about them from reading the papers."

"Really? And yet she raved about you."

"Well I guess you do get a reputation after a while." He drummed his fingers together silently, then rearranging them in the confessional pose. "We opened this firm twenty years ago. There's been a lot of traffic through these doors."

I took a quick look around his office: tan walls, Belle Époque furniture and a series of documents on the wall that looked like The Constitution and the Bill of the Rights, the originals.

"You must get an awful lot of big clients," I said, a patent attempt at flattery.

"We get our share," he nodded.

"Didn't you handle Donald Trump's last divorce?"

"Donald is a client. And a friend."

"He never should have married that girl," I said.

"Which one?" he replied, with a smile. Finally!

"Are you handling Lev Strasser's divorce?" I asked, going for broke.

He gave me a very cool look, but it seemed like the look was a cover for some genuine surprise on his part. In any case, he took a few moments before he responded. And when he did, the response couldn't have been more lawyerly.

"We never discuss our clients' business at this firm," he said.

"So then Lev is a client of yours?"

He cleared his throat, obviously annoyed at me. "What I should say, Mrs. Tyler, is that we never discuss our clients or our business. That's our policy, always has been."

"Oh, look," I replied, as casually as if I had asked about the weather, "I was only asking because Lev is my agent. I figured that he could be a reference."

"Well if he's your agent, why don't you speak to him directly?" The subject was clearly closed.

I leaned back in my chair and tossed off one of those phony laughs I learned to do when I made all those bad movies for Joel in the 80s. "Oh, you know, it's like my ex-husband used to say. Divorce is the bake sale of Beverly Hills."

Which, the moment I said it, I realized was idiotic of me. Leuup's eyes narrowed in two tiny slits.

"I thought you came here to discuss business, Mrs. Tyler," he said.

"I did."

"But you just referred to your ex-husband."

"Yes, I did." Damn, I was trapped.
"Tell me, Mrs. Tyler, are you already divorced?"
I grabbed my purse and stood up.
"Yes, I am. From reality."
And I left.

8

I waved to Inez, who was on the phone, on my way out of Leuup and Spangler and walked right past the elevator station. I mean why risk it? I opened the emergency exit to the staircase and clattered down five flights of stairs. Opening the door to the lobby, I heard my cell phone ring.

"Hello?"

"Nikki, it's Beverly."

"Oh hi," I said as I walked past the security guard I had talked to earlier.

"Where are you?"

"I'm in Century City. Where are you?"

"Perfect," said Beverly. "I'm at Hilda Mazur's. Why don't you come on over and get a facial with me?"

"Well I really hadn't been planning on that." Why was Beverly calling me?

"Nikki," she said, lowering her voice, "I need to talk to you."

"At Hilda's?"

"It's private. No one will disturb us."

"This is important?"

"Would I call you if it weren't?"

"Give me ten minutes."

I had no idea what Beverly wanted to talk to me about, but after our lunch at the Polo Lounge yesterday I was curious, even if the cost of the conversation was going to be a very expensive facial. You can't get any other kind at Hilda Mazur's Skin Clinic since Hilda is the most renowned skin aesthetician in the city. Celebrities put on a scarf and sunglasses and slip through her doors to get their faces slathered, massaged and creamed into glowing good health. Her anti-aging formula goes for over two hundred bucks for a bottle, a tiny bottle, and that's without the detoxifying seaweed gel that no reasonable female movie star would pass up. A few men use it too. I mean, there's a reason why George Clooney looks as good as he does.

So I hopped in my car and drove all of five minutes from Century City to Rodeo Drive. The skyscrapers disappeared and suddenly I was in the heart of the Beverly Hills shopping district, where you can buy a $3,000 cashmere sweater or walk around the corner and get a Jamba Juice. The Mazur Skin Clinic, two stories of light blue mirrored glass, is right next to an art gallery that was having a show of prehistoric artifacts. It was a good bet that there would be a few of those behind the Clinic's door as well.

The receptionist greeted me and led me to the cubicle where Beverly was getting her facial. On the way, I passed Hilda and waved. She was on the phone, but that was just as well. Hovering somewhere between sixty and eternity, Hilda's a tough Hungarian lady whose high pressure sales tactics have caused some to call her the Attila the Hun of cold cream. A while ago a customer, an actress in one of those interchangeable CSI series, complained that Hilda's Skin Rejuvenation Gel wasn't bringing any color to her cheeks, even at $250 an ounce. Hilda raised her hand, slapped the startled girl twice across the face, and said "There's your color, sweetheart. Now get out!" The actress filed a complaint with the Beverly Hills Police Dept., the papers had a field day with it, and a settlement was discreetly reached.

Beverly was reclining on a lounge chair as So Hyun, a Korean woman who's been Hilda's head clinician for years, ministered to her.

"Take off your panty hose and spread out," commanded Beverly. She then turned to So Hyun. "She'll have a facial too. Put it on my tab."

A free facial at Hilda Mazur is something no woman would refuse so I leaned back and So Hyun began to apply a series of cool creams to my cheeks and forehead. My skin began to tingle as her fingers worked the lushly perfumed potions into my flesh. It was wonderful: Haagen-Dazs for the face.

An attendant came in with two Diet Cokes for us, a green straw in each can. $150 for a facial and Hilda couldn't provide a glass and some ice? Then So Hyun left and Beverly and I were alone in the cubicle.

"Feeling good?" she asked.

"Oh yes," I replied. We were both reclining in our lounge chairs, staring at the ceiling. A light pattern, flickering feathers of aqua and pink, washed over it as New Age music played in the background.

"When Joel and I were kids we used to get totally ripped and go to Laserium at the Museum of Natural History back in New York. You know, that big light show they projected on the dome of the Planetarium while they played Pink Floyd's *Dark Side of the Moon*? This is bringing it all back."

"You have lots of memories with Joel," I said carefully.

"Of course I do. We were married for more than twenty years."

"Tyler and I only made it to fourteen. But that's practically a lifetime in rock and roll."

"I don't know how you managed it, Nikki. Being married to a lead singer. And a heavy metal singer! Every night he's screaming out nursery rhymes to an audience of crackheads."

"It's like living next to an airport. After a while you stop hearing the planes take off."

"Joel used to say to me that a movie star is just a rock star who's been toilet trained. And I used to say to him, "You should have stayed a magician.""

"The men we marry," I sighed.

"Yeah, they're the same men we divorce."

Silence. We watched the colored feathers of light undulating above us.

"Did you call me here to talk about Tamara?"

"No."

"She used to come here, you know."

"Of course I know that. Hilda used to have to schedule us on alternate days so we wouldn't run into each other." Any shopkeeper who wishes to be successful in Beverly Hills had better know the first wives from the trophy wives and how to keep them separate.

"It's sort of ironic, our being here," I said. "After all, Tamara started out in cosmetics. I mean, before she got into acting."

"She didn't get into acting," replied Beverly. "She got into the movies."

"Point taken." I wanted to laugh, but I was afraid my facial mask would crack. "So who are we here to talk about?"

"Wendy Strasser."

That got my attention. "Do you know where she is?"

"No, but I know something about her."

"What? Don't play games with me, Beverly."

She lowered her voice to be certain that no one could hear her. "Wendy Strasser has been having an affair."

"Who told you?"

"Rita Collins."

"Why didn't you tell me this when I had lunch with you and Rita yesterday?"

Beverly let out a low chuckle, something mid-way between a laugh and growl. Maybe her facial mask would break.

"Well I really couldn't tell you then because Rita's been having an affair with the same guy."

"You're kidding!" I felt deliciously cheap and trashy, trading this gossip in an overpriced Beverly Hills facial salon like I was a character in one of my own novels.

"Well, maybe not having an affair with him now, but she *had* an affair with him. And she still pines for him. You know Rita, she's the kind that gets attached. So she was very upset when she learned that she'd been replaced by Wendy."

"Who is this himbo?" I asked. "I might want to meet him."

"That's the intriguing part," continued Beverly. "Rita got a bit tipsy last weekend when the two of us went out for a Divorcee's Dinner and she opened up about the affair. But I couldn't get her to tell me the name of the guy. Mostly I think because she wants to get him back, so she doesn't want everyone in town to know about it."

"Well what would be wrong with people knowing about it? Rita's single now. She's entitled to have a fling."

Beverly's voice lowered to a whisper, which made everything sound even nastier than it was. "That's the good part. She started fooling around with this guy when she was married to Palmer."

"No!"

"Yes!"

"And here I thought their marriage broke up because he was fooling around with the actress who played the Virgin Mary in his movie!"

"Daria Belson?"

"Yes, that's her." I just couldn't be bothered to watch "Entertainment Tonight" to keep up with this week's latest starlet.

"There's another one who never got into acting," said Beverly. "But you're right, that's why Palmer left Rita, he wanted to go off with Daria. But learning that Rita was stepping out on him made it a lot easier for him to file the divorce petition against her."

"So Rita wanted the divorce too?"

"I don't think so." Beverly reached out for her Diet Coke and took a long sip. "I think she wanted the marriage plus the screwing on the side from the boy toy. There's only so much you can ask a person, so I can't be sure. But what she did tell me was that she had been nuts for this guy and then he dumped her. So she was devastated when she learned he had taken up with Wendy."

"How did she find out about Wendy and the guy?"

Beverly waved her hand in the air. "I don't know. She probably heard about it at a place like this. Come on, Nikki, it's Beverly Hills. Everybody talks. That's probably why she didn't want to tell me his name."

"This must have been a big factor in her divorce," I said, thinking out loud.

"Oh yeah, but not the way she wanted it to be. Rita clams up about it, but I know for a fact she didn't get that much in the settlement."

"After all that money Palmer made with that ridiculous Nativity movie?"

"They all get greedy after the first ten million," said Beverly grimacing. "Besides, Palmer hired Warren Leuup. The "Jaws" of divorce."

Warren Leuup again! Something was happening over there in that office at Century City. I had to have that lunch with Inez as soon as possible.

"So you think this all has something to do with the fact that Wendy's not around?" I asked Beverly.

She shrugged. "Beats me. Back in Flatbush my father always told me there are two questions: Is it a fish? And if it is, does it stink?"

I turned to Beverly. "Where do you think Wendy could be? Off with the boy toy somewhere?"

She shrugged again. "I just wanted to tell you. You found Tamara. You've been on the news. Wendy's not around. Rita told me this. I figured you should know."

The cubicle's curtain parted and Hilda made her entrance. That's the kind of thing she was good at.

"How are my two favorite people in the entire world?" she asked. Hilda faked sincerity better than most people out here.

"We're fine, Hilda," said Beverly. "Just catching up on things. Girl talk."

"I wish I could join you, but we've been so busy here. Everybody wants an appointment, and then some of them don't want to pay. Do you know that little bitch Laci Stivers asked for a free treatment last week because she said all the paparazzi following her here was good press? And all the time she's yapping about that crazy cult she's a member of. I told her she could take her face and stick it where it belongs, in Hitler's dead crotch."

I told you Hilda wasn't to be trifled with.

"But you two," she continued. "With you I'm not worried. Real ladies, class, that's what Hilda Mazur's is all about. Do you need anything to take home? Some exfoliating gel or our new Artichoke cleansing rinse? The extract comes right from the heart of the artichoke."

"Put a bottle on my bill," said Beverly. It was easier to give into Hilda's sales pitch than resist. You didn't want to wind up on her enemies list, like Laci or the CSI actress.

"By the way, ladies, do either of you know where Wendy Strasser is? She has a standing appointment for Tuesdays and she never misses it. But yesterday she didn't show up, and there was no phone call, no explanation."

We both shook our heads.

"Well, she's going to have to pay anyway," said Hilda sternly. "That's our policy when you don't cancel 24 hours before. It's going to cost her five hundred. I'm not running a soup kitchen here." She reached over, grabbed our Diet Coke cans and disappeared back behind the curtain.

Beverly turned to me. "It's a fish,' she said. "And I think it's beginning to stink."

9

It was almost six by the time I got back home. A Post-It from Madison waited for me on my computer screen. "Lynn called and I told her you are very close to the end. She will call back tomw. morning. Also, hate to tell you, but a pal at the office tells me *TMZ* may be at the end of the driveway soon, courtesy of the *Huffington Post* piece by Lisa Manning, which you should check out at once. M"

Huffington Post? Lisa Manning?! What were they doing in the same sentence?

I sat down and turned on the computer. Before I went to the site I checked my emails, and there was one from Max. It couldn't have been pithier: "Hey Mom, Stopping by tomorrow, probably spending the night. You didn't kill anyone did you? XXX Max."

So I typed in *HuffingtonPost.com* and there it was, a big, red banner headline that screamed "When Celebrities Bite Back" by Lisa Manning.

I started to read:

"As a local news reporter in Los Angeles for KCLM I've been bitten, bashed, and berated in the course of my daily rounds. Celebrities hate to be reported on, and they aren't shy about letting you know it.

What astonishes me is that they don't realize their misbehavior only makes things worse. Case in point: my reporting of the recent murder of producer Joel Osmond's glamorous wife, Tamara.

Two days ago, stationed outside the crime scene, I approached trash novelist (let's be honest here, folks) Nikki Tyler who was leaving the Osmond house in Beverly Hills. Doing the job that any honest reporter would, I asked Ms. Tyler if the police had turned up any suspects only to be told, in the snappiest manner possible, "Yes, they're looking for a local news reporter."

I can't account for the thinking behind Ms. Tyler's reply, but I have heard from a confidential source close to the investigation that the writer is not in the clear and is, indeed, among a number of people whose motives and whereabouts regarding the Osmond killing are being looked into very closely by the authorities.

And here's the funny thing: I wouldn't have dug as deeply into Ms. Tyler's suspect status had she offered a civil reply to my obligatory question. Her nastiness served as the spur for my investigation.

When will celebrities learn that cooperating with the media is the best way to go? I remember when I asked Cher if she resented being mistaken for a tropical fish and she replied...

I hit the off button and watched my computer screen go black, Lisa Manning's deathless prose disappearing back into the cyber netherworlds.

"Being looked into very closely by the authorities!" "Trash novelist!" (Well, okay, but that still puts me about ten steps ahead of "local news reporter.") Damned if that harpy hadn't made me pay in spades for trying to duck her. And what was Arianna doing posting this stuff on her website? I mean, hadn't I bought a whole pan of baklava at her kid's school bake sale? I picked up my cell phone and speed dialed her.

"Hello darling, this is Arianna. Who's calling?"

"Arianna, it's Nikki Tyler."

"Nikki, darling, how good to hear from you. How are you?"

Not so good since I read the story on your website."

"What's the matter, darling? Have we endorsed a Republican?"

"Forget the Republicans, Arianna. You've got a story naming me as a suspect in Tamara's Osmond's murder!"

"Oh that's impossible. I know you wouldn't kill anyone, Nikki. Outside of a few book reviewers."

"Take a look at the website, it's your lead story. And it's by that bleached blond terrorist Lisa Manning."

"Lisa's on our website? Really? I wouldn't even pose for a Christmas card with that girl."

"I'm getting emails from everyone I know, Arianna." I hated being a whiner, but this was special.

"You know, darling, I'm not at home right now. I'm in Washington lobbying some of the senators about the carbon emissions bill. My associates are running the site. I'll have to look into this later. Right now I'm late for a meeting with Dianne Feinstein. Is there anything you'd like me to tell her for you?

"Yes. Tell her I'm not guilty!"

"I love you, Nikki," cooed Arianna like she meant it, which she does since Arianna loves everyone. "Let's have lunch at the Polo Lounge when I get back. The McCarthy salad."

I turned off my cell phone and tried to find a place for my rage. Breaking dishes? Nah, too easy. Kicking the furniture? Might break a heel. So I turned to the old reliable, baking. I don't know about you, but nothing calms me down as quickly as heading into the kitchen, pulling out the pans, and baking up a high calorie treat I can feast on later.

Tonight I needed something very special, so I settled on Katharine Hepburn's Brownies. They're the best brownies I've ever tasted, made with very little flour so they just barely make it across the border from fudge. I'm not giving the recipe here because, as I told Rita at the Polo Lounge, I don't write that kind of book. So if you want it, check the internet and you'll find a least a dozen listings.

When I was finished I let them cool for an hour, an essential step by the way, went back to the computer and answered all the emails that had piled up during the day. Then I took the pan of brownies to bed with me and ate almost half of it while I looked through Tamara's book again for clues. Still no luck.

Morning came, the phone rang and I reached across the nightstand, past the half-eaten Katharine Hepburn Brownies, picked up the receiver and found Lynn on the other end.

"Hello love," she chirped all the way from New York. "Madison tells me you're almost through with the book."

I looked down at the copy of "Revenge of the Trophy Wives," which I had apparently kicked to the floor during the night. "Well, yes, but it's not my book I seem to be finishing."

"How's that?"

I sighed and leaned back on the pillows the way those ladies used to do on *Dynasty* all those years ago. "It's so complicated, Lynn. Joel Osmond asked me to read this chick lit book Tamara wrote, and I did, and then she got killed. I've been looking in the book for clues ever since."

"Come up with anything?"

"Not yet. Just a lot of bad writing about shoes and sex."

There was a pause on the other end. I could practically hear Lynn thinking.

"Nikki," she said softly, "is this something I should be looking at?"

I sat up in bed. "Lynn, you mean you would consider publishing it?"

"In today's market, it's a possibility. We're always looking for something with an angle, and a murder is a big angle. Plus the fact that it might hold clues to who killed her. Why that's practically out of "The Da Vinci Code!"

"Okay, fine. I'll send it to you and you can publish it. Forget *Malibu Bad Boy*, you can just stick my name on the cover of Tamara's book as a co-author. Everybody's doing that nowadays. Why bother to write anything?"

Lynn picked up on my hurt immediately. "Nikki, please. I said the wrong thing. I'm dying to read *Malibu* as soon as you finish it."

That helped. "Thanks, Lynn. I don't mean to be touchy, but things are getting crazy out here."

"That's why I called, love. I've read the *Huffington Post*, I've been watching TV, and I know the stress you're under. I called to tell you not to worry. Take the time you need to finish the book you want to write. We can wait. We'll always be here for you."

Nothing makes an insecure author feel better than to hear her publishing house grovel just a wee bit. I scraped my index finger through the brownie pan and licked off the lovely residue.

"You're sweet, Lynn."

"Forget what I said about the Osmond book. You know, sometimes working in publishing seems like the easiest way to forget what books are really about: people picking up something they've never seen before and losing themselves in another world."

"That's why I used to read when I was a kid." *I also used to eat brownies at the same time,* I thought to myself. Nothing changes, it just gets more expensive.

Lynn sighed on the other end. She was letting her professional mask drop, always a good sign.

"Nikki, you wouldn't believe what we're asked to consider here by top management. Anything with a celebrity name on it gets published, no questions asked. And just last week we got the word that we're publishing a history of erectile dysfunction during the American Revolution."

"What?"

"Marketing came up with what they think is a brilliant title."

"Which is?"

"*And Called it Macaroni.*"

I burst out laughing. "Oh Lynn, who wrote this thing?"

"Some conservative historian who claims he had bad sex with Anne Coulter. They think they can book him on the talk shows with that angle."

"Well if that's all it takes to get published, I'm sure you'll have hundreds of potential authors at your doorstep."

"Nikki, take your time. Do what you have to do, and we'll deal with the book when you're ready."

"Thanks, Lynn. I love you."

"You too, love."

Our conversation reminded me of what it was I liked so much about Lynn: her candor. Years ago I wrote my first book, a silly Civil War romance. Max had just started school, Tyler was out on tour, and when I wasn't packing school lunches I passed the time by reading romance novels. After about the tenth one, I figured I could do better. A friend of a friend "knew somebody" at a publishing house, so my little effort, "Love's Savage Slavery," was passed onto her. The somebody turned out to be Lynn.

I still remember what she said in her rejection letter. "Dear Nikki Tyler, Although your writing shows promise, I'm not sure that the Civil War is your subject. Are you the Nikki Tyler who's married to Travis Tyler? If so, a novel about your take on Hollywood might be just the ticket. Regards, Lynn Mosson."

That was the note that sent me to the computer to write "Madam Hollywood," the story of a Beverly Hills doctor's daughter who starts an escort service and winds up with half the male stars in Hollywood as her johns. Pure fiction, of course. I made the New York Times best seller list with the book, and Lynn and I have been joined at the hip ever since.

I took a quick shower and pulled on a pair of sweat pants and an old top. Despite what Lynn had said, I wanted to try to finish my book. But as I sat down at my desk, the brownie pan at my side, I heard a car pulling into the driveway. When I answered the door, my ex-husband was waiting there.

"Hello, babe," he said with that smile that had made my knees buckle more than two decades ago. "Can I come in?"

"Of course," I said as we made our way to the study. Travis was in his veteran rock star attire, tight black jeans, a white Hanes T-shirt, and a diamond stud earring. He still had his hair and, from the looks of the T-shirt, he still had his six pack. And here I was dressed like I was waiting for menopause or the plumber, or both. Damn.

"What's up?" I asked as we sat down. "Why didn't you call?"

He shrugged and gave me that rock guy smile that's worked on so many of us over the years. "I just figured we could talk like this, you know, one to one." He paused. "Man to woman."

"Primate to primate," I said. Something was clearly on his mind.

"Oh, the brownies," he exclaimed, reaching over and grabbing one of the few left in the pan. "I miss these suckers." Two bites and it was gone.

Silence.

"Travis, why are you here?" It felt just a bit odd to have him in the house. That's how it goes with exes, I guess.

"I wanted to talk to you about the nursery school for Divinity," he replied, shifting in his chair, trying to get comfortable.

"But we already talked about that. I told you to have Heidi call me."

"There are some problems, babe." He looked at me guiltily, the way Max did the first time I caught looking at porn on his computer. "Heidi found this great place in Brentwood, Montessori, multi-racial, the whole bit. Eddie Murphy's kids go there, even the illegitimate ones. Everything was set. But then they turned us down."

"I hope there was no problem with Divinity?" I said. You're always protective of your kids, so I couldn't help but feel for Heidi.

"No, Divinity's fine. They liked her."

"Then what's the problem?"

"You."

"Me!" What the hell could I have to do with getting Travis' daughter accepted at some tony nursery school?

"They were upset that we were married and now you're all over the internet and the papers with this murder case. They don't like the negative publicity, said they were afraid they might have news crews coming to the school, trying to get footage, stuff like that."

"That's ridiculous!" I exclaimed. "Why would they want pictures of you and your daughter just because you used to be married to me?"

Travis hitched his thumb over his shoulder. "Check outside, babe. The sharks are circling."

I went over to window, pulled the curtain back and saw a news van, a cameraman and a soundman. Madison's pals from *TMZ*, I was sure.

I felt exasperated and overwhelmed at the same time. "I don't control the media, Travis. I can't help it if a bunch of morons with microphones want to follow me around. But they're not going to follow you. This school is totally overreacting."

"It's a very exclusive place. They're concerned about their reputation."

"Right!" I fumed. "That's why they've enrolled all the little bastards of the stars."

"I think they might have gotten burned during the O.J. thing," said Travis. "Anyway, they said they would have to pass on Divinity as long as you were a suspect in this murder case."

"I am NOT a suspect!" I said jumping out of my chair. "Why the hell does everybody seem to think I could have murdered Tamara?"

Travis looked at me as he reached over and grabbed another brownie. "Jealousy?" he said.

And that did it. The dam burst and I began to cry, tears rolling down my cheeks, sob backing up in my throat. "Leave those goddamned brownies alone!" I shrieked. "They're mine!"

Travis came up from his chair in one swift motion and wrapped his arms around me. "Babe." He pressed my head into his chest. "Calm down. It's all right. I promise you, it's all right."

I gave myself a minute to let my tears subside, my face crushed against his T-shirt. He smelled just like he had during our 14 years of marriage; some things never leave you. I pulled back and wiped away the last of my tears.

"God, I'm sorry." I felt really embarrassed now, the kind of embarrassed that takes you all the way back to grade school when you were the only girl at the lunch table who didn't know what a period was.

"Babe," he said, "it happens." Travis released me from his grip and I began to feel like an adult again.

"The past few days have just been a nightmare, what with finding Tamara in the kitchen and now all this news coverage and the emails and phone calls I'm getting. Why would anyone think I would be a suspect in this case?"

"'Cause they're dumb?"

"Yes!" I said. "Idiots, all of them. And I just overreacted to what you said. Sorry for all the tears and the shouting."

"Hey, no problem," said Travis. "It's just like old times.'

I grabbed the brownie pan and shoved it at him. "Here, eat the rest of these. Go ahead, they're yours."

He laughed and held his hands in the air. "Babe, I'm not going near the Hepburn Brownies when you're in a bad mood. I know what's good for me."

I tossed them back on the desk. "I just need to decompress. I've been spending too much time on this murder. Talking to people, looking for Wendy Strasser. It's stressed me out."

"Where's Wendy?" Travis had gotten to know her during the week she was married to Rod Stewart.

"Wish I knew," I replied. "She and Tamara were so involved in this book that Tamara wrote, and now no one can find her."

"Have you asked Lonny?" said Travis.

Lonny Pardo had been the drummer in Nausea when band first formed. Part musician, part madman, he was a total sex fiend. Travis used to like to say that Lonny had been in more women than the IUD.

"Why would Lonny Pardo know where Wendy is?" I asked.

Travis smiled at my ignorance. "He was having a little thing with her last year. Just a bit of afternoon delight, nothing serious. But I think he got to know her pretty well."

"Where is he?"

"Where do you think he'd be?"

"In rehab," I said.

Travis' smile got bigger. "I'll give you the address," he said.

10

Remember what I told you about olives and dirty martinis? Well, learning that Lonny was in rehab was an olive, an unexpected bit of good news that could help me find Wendy and clear my name. But it was more than. If used properly, it might even improve my social life. And I'd be lying if I said that wasn't part of what I was thinking about when I called Detective Stefano with the news.

"He knows where Mrs. Strasser is?" he said after I told him about Lonny.

"Well, according to my ex, he got to know her fairly… intimately," I replied.

"And where is Mr. Pardo now?"

"He's taking a rest. But I can get us in to see him."

Half an hour later the good Detective roared up to my door on his Harley Davidson. He was wearing Cargo Shorts and a yellow golf shirt. I'd had just enough time to change into a tennis outfit.

"You're looking informal," I said.

He shrugged. "My day off. I was on my way to go racing when you called me."

"You don't mind working when you're off duty?"

"Not when I'm on a case. Where are we headed?"

"To Malibu." I looked down the driveway and saw the news van. "But first we have to get past them."

"Piece of cake," he said as I locked the door and we walked towards his Harley. "You ever ride on the back of a motorcycle?"

"Hey, I was married to a rock star. I've done a lot of things."

"Great. Hop on."

He gunned the motor four times in a row and then we took off with the sound of tires squealing against the driveway. The cameraman and the sound guy scattered like the cockroaches they were as we roared out the driveway and onto the street. I let out a whoop and waved to one of my neighbors who stared in disbelief as she was unloading her groceries. I mean, hey, live free or die, right?

We turned onto Sunset and I felt the wind against my face as the Detective—I wasn't calling him Rocco yet—pushed it to fifty, swooping around the Sunset Pass, the treacherous quarter mile of the Boulevard that dips down and loops around as you head to the Bel Air Gate. The houses and trees flew by me in a blur and I held tight to the seat handle, hooking my right hand into the band of his shorts for good measure. Yes, like they used to say at Weight Watchers, this was living.

"You okay back there?" he shouted.

"I'm fine," I screamed back. "I used to do this with Robert Downey Jr. Before he went into rehab."

Now we were on Pacific Coast Highway, the ocean on one side of us, mansions on the other. The heady scent of the sea air actually managed to overpower the stench of all those transmissions, and the sun felt glorious on my back. Like most Los Angelinos do when they get to the beach, I marveled that I live less than 30 minutes away from all this but almost never visit it.

Just about a mile past Paradise Cove we took a left and the detective steered the bike into the driveway of New Beginnings. That's the kind of fancy, New Age name they give to rehab centers out here, although this one made almost no sense to me. Have you ever heard of an *old* beginning? Anyway, New Beginnings was a pretty posh deal, a big Greco-Roman villa, with a huge stone terrace that overlooked the Pacific. That's where we found Lonny.

The best definition I ever heard of addiction is that it's something you keep doing over and over even though you get the same bad result every time. I was at a Phoenix House fundraiser in Bel Air years ago when I repeated that and Dame Elizabeth Taylor turned to me and said, "Isn't that the definition of marriage?" Everyone laughed, but later on Dame Elizabeth came over to me and asked me if I had a problem. Happily I didn't, but, being around rock and roll, I'd known enough people who had. Besides, when you get right down to it, we're all addicted to something. Some of us just got lucky and wound up with an addiction to a substance as harmless as brownies.

All of which is my way of telling you that, yes, I saw several people you probably know at New Beginnings, but I'm not going to repeat their names. If someone is trying to turn their life around, they deserve respect, not gossip. Why they got here in the first place is the big question. Some starred on television, others once made hit records; but all of them had had a brush with one of the deadliest viruses I know of: celebrity. They had been known and now they weren't. Or they were still known, but had discovered that it wasn't enough. Either way, that blows a big hole in your life, and lots of people use drugs or alcohol to plaster over that hole.

From what I remember of Lonny, he had probably used both when he was doing his plastering. In any case, he was so startled to see me, I felt I had sobered him up right on the spot.

"Nikki! What in the hell are you doing here?" he said as we approached him. Lonny had shaved all his hair off and was wearing a T-shirt that read "Drummers Die First."

"I came to visit, Lonny. Travis told me you were here."

He looked over at Detective Stefano, then back at me. "Did you get married again?"

The detective stuck out his hand. "I'm Rocco Stefano with the L.A.P.D. I'd like to talk with you about something, if you have a minute."

Lonny threw his hands out in front of him. "Now lookit," he said. "We were just playing around. Neither one of us meant any harm. I'd just always wondered if Magic Glue really could make you stick to anything. And then when I got stuck, well, I reached for the crackpipe to melt the glue. Nobody got hurt. Although I did lose almost all my pubic hair."

"Lonny." I reached over and took his hand. "Like the song says, 'You've got to change your evil ways.'"

"I know, Nikki." He hung his head a bit. "That's why I'm back in rehab. You know what they say, fourth time's the charm."

"It's not a game, Lonny," I said. "We're not in our twenties anymore."

"Tell me about. I feel like I've got stretch marks on my balls."

If any of this disturbed Detective Stefano, he didn't let it show. "Mr. Pardo, we're here to ask you about a friend of yours."

"I don't have many friends left," Lonny fretted.

"I'm wondering if you can tell us anything about Wendy Strasser?"

Lonny looked over at me. "Is Wendy in trouble?"

"Not trouble," I said. "But nobody can find her. We thought you might be able to help."

"Hell, I haven't seen her in about a year. One of those things, you know? Over and out."

"You haven't spoken to her recently?" asked Detective Stefano. "No phone calls, text messages, anything like that?"

Lonny shook his head. "There was no reason for that. I pretty much got the idea that Wendy had moved on to somebody new." Which, of course, was just what Beverly had told me yesterday at Hilda Mazur's.

Detective Stefano pulled out his pad. "Any idea who that could be?"

"Not really," Lonny replied. "But I'll bet you he was younger than me. Wendy was a lady with appetites, if you know what I mean."

Stefano grinned and nodded. Guy talk, of course he knew what Lonny meant. But then, so did I.

"Weren't you worried about being caught by Lev?" I asked. "He's got a ferocious temper."

"Hell." Lonny snorted. "That bald bastard was too busy making money to have any idea what his wife was doing during the day. Besides, we used to meet up in a private place of Wendy's that he didn't know a thing about."

"Where was that?" Stefano asked.

"Little apartment up in Laurel Canyon. It's a converted garage, behind a home that some old lady owns. Wendy rented the place when she first got here years ago and never gave up the lease. She used to call it her love shack."

Detective Stefano was hanging on every word. "Remember the address?"

"714 ½ Wonderland Avenue." Lonny smiled at the memory. "We had some damn good afternoons up there."

I thought of how cool Wendy had seemed when I'd had lunch with her and Tamara at Barneys. She really had the trophy wife act down pat, the shopping, the facials, the charity luncheons Never a hair out of place, and never an extra pound on her frame. And yet all the while she'd been two-timing Lev with a series of studs. And cut rate studs at that, to judge by Lonny. *Maybe she was the inspiration for Tamara's novel*, I thought to myself. *And maybe that's why she is missing?* Could she have murdered Tamara? It wasn't a stretch to think Wendy was capable of murder.

Lonny's voice snapped me back to reality. "Hey, Nikki, you planning on doing any more acting?"

"No," I laughed. "I've decided to give Meryl Streep a break."

"You ought to think about it," insisted Lonny. "I saw *Bathsheba, Queen of Blood* the other night on cable and you were good."

"I'm writing, Lonny. It's a better living and you don't have to worry about being too old. The computer's a lot more forgiving than the camera."

"You've still got some connections though, right? You're still in the business?"

"Lonny, out here it's all business. Do you need some help with something?"

Lonny looked around at the terrace, at the former sitcom stars, athletes, and singers who had put aside all the bad little toys and were now on their First Step.

"Do you think I could get a reality show out of this?" he asked.

* * * *

We took Sunset back into town, the wind still whipping around us as we darted through the mid-day traffic. Racing past UCLA, Detective Stefano drove between two BMWs and I was sure we were going to wind up as roadkill.

"You feel like a cheeseburger?" he shouted as we left the twin Beemers in the dust.

"I feel like a middle aged woman on the back of a motorcycle," I screamed back. "But I'll eat anything to get off this bike."

We pulled into everybody's favorite fast food place in Southern California, In 'N Out Burger. The burgers come stuffed with pickles and onions and wrapped in paper, and the shoestring fries are almost better than sex. It's the Polo Lounge for real people. Over cheeseburgers and Diet Cokes, the Detective started to cross examine me.

"So you were an actress. You never told me that."

"I'd hardly call it acting. As a friend of mine likes to say, "I didn't get into acting, I got into the movies." There's a difference."

He wiped his mouth and grabbed a handful of French fries. "Still, that's pretty cool. I was an actor for a while before I got into police work."

"You're kidding." I was genuinely surprised; he just didn't seem the type. "Were you in anything I might have seen?"

"Just direct to video. It's a long story."

"Well, I'd love to hear it. I mean, who would have ever thought you were an actor?"

He dismissed it with a shrug. "Like I said, it's a long story."

"I love long stories," I countered. "After all, I'm a novelist."

"I'd rather hear about your career." He closed the subject.

"I spent more time at parties with the Brat Pack than I did acting. I wasn't really serious about it, and I was too young to realize that."

He grinned and raised his eyebrows. "The Brat Pack, huh?"

"Now you're going to tell me you had a big thing for Demi Moore. Well just let me warn you she's an old pal, and I don't like people dissing her."

"She wasn't my style. I liked Kathleen Turner more."

"Oh God, yes! *Body Heat*! She was amazing." I reached for a fistful of fries in honor of Kathleen.

"I've always gravitated more towards older women."

Bingo!

He just let the remark hang there, and I decided to say nothing. The last thing I wanted to do was push it with the first really interesting, attractive guy I'd met in ages. Two months ago my mother had set me up with the son of a Palm Springs friend of hers, a plastic surgeon from Brentwood. We spent the evening at a retro fondue place, dunking cubes of bread in gunky cheese while he told me how he'd just done a brow lift on a 78 year old Jehovah's Witness who wanted to look good for the Endtimes. This lunch represented a distinct step up for me.

"Are you going to Laurel Canyon?" I asked.

He nodded. "Want to come along?"

"Is that legal?"

"Technically, I'm off duty. And since you're a friend of Mrs. Strasser, it might be useful to have you with me."

"You got a deal."

We got back on the bike, back onto Sunset, and a few minutes later we were riding up the twisting roads of Laurel Canyon. Despite all the SUVs and the tear downs, there were still enough funky old houses, wind chimes hanging on their front porches, to remind me that Joni Mitchell and lots of other peace and love types lived here in the late sixties. Laurel Canyon has always been more of an enclave than most other L.A. neighborhoods.

We parked across from 714 Wonderland Avenue, a crumbling two story affair covered in ancient brown shingles that were, in turn, covered with some very tired looking ivy. Heavy muslin curtains covered all the windows. Perhaps Joni Mitchell was still inside, like Miss Havisham, sitting in her hippie wedding gown waiting for Crosby or Stills or Nash, or possibly even Young.

"Stay behind me," Detective Stefano ordered as we walked down the gravel driveway to the garage. A staircase on the side of it led to a small second story landing and a door. The address 730 ¼ was spelled out next to the door in rusty silver numerals, the ¼ hanging upside down, held by only one small nail.

And why did I notice all this? Because I was scared to death and you would have been too. Who the hell knew what we were going to find behind that door?

11

The first thing that hit me after we walked into the apartment, after the Detective tried to jimmy the lock and discovered that he didn't have to, that the door was already unlocked, was the stench. It was overpowering, rank and foul, far more pungent than rotting food. I put my hand over my face and coughed. The apartment was just a small living room with a kitchen off of it. That's where the smell was coming from.

Which wasn't surprising, because that's where Wendy's body was, slumped up against the wall, next to the stove.

I gasped when I saw it and grabbed the detective's arm.

He steadied me, but I had seen the worst already. There were two bullet wounds in Wendy's chest and her eyes were half open, almost as if she was looking up to see who had done this to her. And somebody surely had. Somebody was killing the trophy wives of Beverly Hills, and in their kitchens, no less.

A bullet casing lay on the tile floor. The Detective knelt, pulled a paper clip out of his pocket, unbent it and picked up the shell up with it. He held it aloft and studied it.

"Nine millimeter, from a handgun," he said. "Probably a Ruger."

"And what's a Ruger?"

"The same type of gun that killed Tamara Osmond."

I looked over at Wendy, struggling to believe what I saw. The bullet wounds had created blood stains in the blue jersey top she was wearing. Her tight jeans were cinched with that belt she'd bought at Barneys, and she was wearing her trusty old Ugg Boots. She looked like she was ready to go somewhere. Only someone had stopped her.

"Do you think the same person killed them?' I was feeling stunned and scared and nauseous, but most of all I was curious. The Detective leaned over, inspected Wendy's corpse, and even sniffed the air like a dog.

"She's been dead for a few days," he said, standing back up. "The body hasn't begun to decompose yet, but it's released its fluids, its toxins. That's normal. And that's what you're smelling."

"That's okay," I said. "I can take it. I'm an adult."

He turned and looked at me very seriously. "You don't understand. This is a crime scene. You have to leave. We'll take a statement later."

His authority was absolute; I knew I had to comply. "I'll call a cab."

"Before you do, one thing."

"Yes?"

He leaned back over and looked at Wendy's face again.

"Can you tell me why Mrs. Strasser would be wearing the same kind of earring that Mrs. Osmond was when she killed?"

Damned if he wasn't right. Wendy had the same gold hoop monkey earring in her left ear that Tamara had had in hers. The same earrings that Chloe had worn at the Polo Lounge. And, like Tamara, she was in the kind of thrown together outfit that just didn't work for her.

"I have no clue," I replied. "None at all."

"Get yourself a cab and get home," said the detective as he pulled out his cell phone and started dialing. "I'll get homicide and the coroner over here, and I'll call you later."

He was all business now; this was his profession. I headed towards the door, practically stumbling over two suitcases, one Luis Vuitton, the other Coach, that were next to it. Was Wendy going somewhere?

I dialed a cab as I went down the staircase. When I reached the driveway a white haired woman in a flower print housedress stepped out of the back door of the house. She could have passed for anybody's grandmother except for the pistol she held in her hand. It was carefully pointed directly at me.

"What the hell are you doing on my property?" she demanded.

Instinctively I raised my hands, trying to show that I was in no way a threat to her. "I was looking for my friend, Wendy Strasser. She's supposed to live back here."

"If she's your friend, you ought to know where she is." The grim-faced old woman kept the gun trained on me.

I was petrified. I thought of screaming out so Detective Stefano would hear me, but I couldn't risk the woman shooting me. We were standing in the middle of the driveway with nothing around us.

"She's been mi...mi...missing," I stuttered, something I hadn't done since middle school, out of pure fear. "No one's seen her for days." I had to hope the old woman wasn't Wendy's killer.

"Well I haven't either," she groused.

"Drop your weapon."

It was Detective Stefano, behind me, on top of the landing. I was too scared to even turn around and take a look at him. The old woman wasn't. She looked up and raised her pistol.

"Who the hell are you?"

"I'm a homicide investigator with the L.A.P.D. and you're in violation of the law right now. Drop your weapon."

The woman looked at him hard, considering her options, and then slowly lowered the pistol. I turned around to see the Detective standing on the landing without a gun in his hand, just an L.A.P.D. badge that he had held up to show her. God, to have guts like that.

"I don't know where the hell that woman is," she said. "She owes me back rent. I've been waiting for it for a week now."

"You should have checked the apartment." The detective came down the stairs and took the gun from her hand. "She's been waiting up there for you."

* * * *

When I got back home, there were two surprises. The camera crew was gone. Maybe we'd scared them away, maybe they'd heard about Wendy's death and were headed over to Laurel Canyon. Either way, I felt free. The second surprise was even nicer; there was a laundry bag in the front hallway.

"Max?" I shouted as I let myself in.

"In here." He was sitting in the living room, texting on his iPhone. I could only hope he worked his courses as hard as he was working the phone.

"Are you here for the weekend?" I asked.

"Uh huh," he said, his eyes not moving from the screen, his fingers scrambling across the keyboard.

"Did you talk to your father about the money for Hawaii?"

"Uh huh." Eyes still glued, fingers still scrambling.

"Do you want me to make the lasagna?"

"Uh huh." Still glued, still scrambling.

"Shall I cut off your penis and put it in the meat sauce?"

"Mom, I can hear everything you're saying. It's not like I can't multi-task, you know? And, uh, no you don't have to put my penis in the sauce. Unless you're gonna dip your breasts in it, like you did in all those lame movies you used to make." He was still texting, of course.

"Beast." I went over and affectionately whacked him on the back of the head. My little Max Monster. I walked into the kitchen, pulled out a frying pan and began sautéing the beef and the onions.

Max joined me.

"How long till it's ready?" he asked.

"About an hour and a half."

79

That brought forth a groan so I grabbed the brownie pan and shoved it across the counter. "Here, why don't you finish these while you wait?"

The long trails my fingernails had made in the brownies resembled irrigation ditches in a farmer's field. "It looks like a family of squirrels has been eating this," he complained.

"Not squirrels," I replied, "but a family. Enjoy." I turned the flame up under the water for the flat noodles.

"So, Mom, you didn't murder Mrs. Osmond?"

"No. And I didn't murder Mrs. Strasser either."

"Mrs. Strasser?"

"Didn't know about that one, did you?"

For the next hour, while I assembled and cooked the lasagna, I told Max everything that had happened. I must have done a good job, because when I was finished he had no questions left, only a ravenous appetite. He had a second helping while I, still on my first, allowed myself a second glass of Pinot Noir. I'd earned it.

"Wow, Mom," said Max as he made a huge slab of noodles, beef and cheese disappear in a single gulp, "I had no idea things were so tough for you."

"Don't talk with your mouth full, Max. I've been telling you that for nineteen years. And don't worry about me. I'll be okay."

"That's cool." His plate was clean now.

"So," I said, "you dating anyone?" The wine had made me feel casual. Max shook his head.

"Interested in anyone?" Okay, I was a nosy mother. Aren't we all?

He smiled at me across the table. "No Mom. Not dating anyone right now. How about you? Are you dating anyone?"

I was tempted to say "stay tuned," but thought better of it. "No," I replied. "So I guess we're even."

"Awesome." He slid his now empty plate into the dishwasher and headed back to the living room. "More texting?" I asked.

"Oh yeah," he replied. "Hey, it's not like I'm ignoring you or anything, right?"

"Right." And, actually, I didn't feel ignored. The wine was paying attention to me: that was enough for right now.

"We'll talk some more at breakfast, okay?" he said.

I shook my head. "I won't be here for breakfast tomorrow."

"How come?"

"I'm going to Tamara Osmond's funeral."

* * * *

If you're Catholic and you die in Beverly Hills, you'll probably wind up having your funeral at the Church of the Good Shepherd, which, the dying part aside, isn't such a bad deal at all. It's the oldest church in Beverly Hills; Frank Sinatra and Alfred Hitchcock had their funerals there. Elizabeth Taylor even got married there, at least the first time around, which, I guess, was sort of a funeral for her.

I was headed to Tamara's service at the Good Shepherd with Tyler and Heidi. They had invited me to attend with them, which was sweet. There's no substitute for a good ex-husband. Tyler and I were both in black, but Heidi had gone for a coral Donna Karan suit. Out here, that's allowed.

"Churches always make me feel so religious," sighed Heidi.

"That's the general idea." I tugged at the hem of my skirt. I was in Donna Karan too. Her stuff always works.

"Did you send any flowers?" asked Travis. "We sent a bouquet."

"I sent some white roses. Tamara always liked roses."

"Our bouquet had lots of daises," said Heidi. "Beautiful cyan daises."

"What? I've never heard of that color."

"It's a very powerful one," she continued. "My color therapist suggested it. Cyan means a calming of the physical. And that's the transition Tamara is going through right now. Her physical energy is being calmed as her spiritual energy takes over."

"Yes," I said, "but what actual color is it?"

"Blue," said Travis, "a very bright sky blue. The kind you used to see on a Chevy Impala back in the sixties."

"And now maybe Tamara can ride that Impala right into heaven," said Heidi.

Cyan, I thought to myself. *How unbelievable.*

"Oh look," cried out Heidi. "Birds!" A small pack of starlings were circling one of the trees on the corner of Bedford Drive where the church was. "God must have sent them for Tamara's funeral."

"That's a beautiful thought, hon." Travis patted her knee.

"It's like they've brought a special blessing with them," she added. After posing naked for millions of readers in Playboy, Heidi had found religion when she and Travis got married. Now she kept her clothes on, but her thinking was definitely off.

"If you think about it," Heidi continued, "birds are really God's confetti."

"If you think about it," I said, trying to be pleasant.

Tyler shot me a quick look as we pulled into the parking lot.

There were about a hundred people in the church. Tamara's parents were dead, but her older sister, Marisa, was there, sitting in the front pew next to Joel. When she began to cry during the service, Joel put his arm around her and held her close. That was Joel, always the producer, always in control. Beverly sat a few rows behind Joel. When she saw us enter the church, she beckoned us over.

"I'm surprised to see you here," I whispered as I sat next to her.

"I'm here for Joel," she said simply.

Rita Collins, sitting on the other side of Beverly, nodded to me. Poor Rita looked pale and drawn, and I couldn't help feeling it didn't just have to do with Tamara's death. Maybe it was the vegetarian diet, maybe it was her rocky love life, but Rita looked like she needed a rest. She grew even paler as her ex-husband Palmer walked in with his new wife, Daria Belson, the former Virgin Mary, on his arm.

There's a way that a movie star enters a room and Palmer, after more than two decades of stardom, had it down. His walk had a spring to it and his face bore a tight, small smile. I'd seen that same smile on Michael Douglas and Harrison Ford. It said, 'yes, you know me and I know that you know me, now can we please just get on with the business at hand?'

Despite his tanned face and perfectly cut auburn hair (dyed, but you couldn't really tell), Palmer had begun to get tiny crow's feet around his eyes, the love handles of aging action stars. But damned if the lines didn't make him look even better; they gave him a kind of aged-in-wood character he hadn't had before. On us they're wrinkles, on them it's character. At fifty five Palmer was no kid, but he didn't look that different from when he had starred in "Salt and Pepper" with Eddie Murphy in the mid-eighties. That buddy picture, with Palmer as a young cop from Mississippi who comes to L.A. and gets partnered with Eddie to track down a racist serial killer, helped chase "Bathsheba, Queen of Blood" out of the multiplexes and into the video stores.

Daria, wearing a gray wool jersey number that had a neckline more appropriate for a lap dance than a funeral, clung to his arm. Oh well, if you've got it flaunt it, I suppose. They wore matching Gucci sunglasses and Palmer had a white carnation in the buttonhole of his Hugo Boss charcoal grey jacket.

He came over to our pew and spoke in the kind of actor's whisper you use to disclose state secrets in the last reel of a movie. Looking past the rest of us, he fixed his gaze on Rita.

"Hello, my wife," he said. My wife! Didn't he have one on his arm already?

"Hello," Rita murmured. She was trying to look at him and ignore Daria at the same time, not easy.

"A shame we have to meet this way."

Rita nodded. Daria shifted uncomfortably, taking her arm out of his.

Palmer took the carnation out of his buttonhole, kissed it and handed it down the aisle to Rita. "Be well," he said.

God almighty, I thought to myself, what's he going for, the Academy Award? That little performance had had everything behind it but a one hundred piece symphony orchestra playing the John Williams title theme song. But it seemed to have worked on Rita; she held the flower tenderly. Palmer and Daria took seats in the pew across the aisle from the rest of us.

I heard the clack-clack-clack of stiletto heels against the church's marble floor and turned to see Chloe and Laci Stivers coming up the aisle together. Chloe looked very subdued, all in black, but Laci, bless her tabloid loving heart, had chosen to wear a hot pink minidress. Maybe she was going to a pool party later. Anyway, it was nice of her to accompany Chloe, who scooted to the other side of Joel and gave him a big hug which he promptly returned.

The service began, and it was just the way you would have wanted it to be if it was your own. There was a lovely opening hymn, Joel read the 23rd Psalm, and then the priest delivered a tender eulogy that helped remind us of the things that had made Tamara so special, her humor, her enthusiasm, her gift for friendship. I couldn't help but wonder if anyone in attendance had heard of Wendy's death. If they had, they didn't mention it.

Half an hour later a young African American woman sang *Amazing Grace* and we were all out on Bedford Drive, chatting in little groups, not wanting to let go of the morning's ceremony.

I was standing next to Joel when Palmer came over with Daria still by his side. He gave him one of those big guy-guy bear hugs.

"This sucks, buddy. Really sucks," he said.

Joel smiled grimly. "Worse things have happened. There's a rumor Madonna may return to acting."

83

Palmer cracked up. "That's the way, Joel. Don't let the bastards get you down."

"You know my motto: Smile when you call me a son of a bitch. And then smile at my mother too."

"Daria and I would love to have you out to the beach house. Maybe you could take a weekend, just sit on the deck with us, watch the waves, have a few margaritas." As Palmer talked I watched Rita out of the corner of my eye. She stared at Laci Stivers, who ignored her the way she had ignored everybody, including God, during the funeral. Chloe stood beside Laci, texting on her iPhone just like Max had the other day.

"That might be nice, Palmer," replied Joel. Even behind his dark glasses, I could see his eyes spark to the idea. Marisa remained at Joel's side, her hand in his, sharing the connection they both felt to Tamara. Beverly stood over to the side, her arms crossed, as if she were waiting her turn. Was it her turn again now that Tamara was gone?

Suddenly Chloe rushed up to Joel, her phone clutched in her hand. "Daddy! Wendy Strasser's been murdered. They found her body yesterday. Look!" She thrust the phone under Joel's gaze as a collective gasp went up from the small crowd.

"Jesus Christ," muttered Joel as his eyes scanned the news item Chloe had found on line. He turned to the rest of us. "Did anybody know about this?"

It was put up or shut up time. "I did, Joel."

"When did you know?"

"Actually I found the body."

"Again?" he asked incredulously.

I could see everyone staring at me, even Laci. I knew I had to tell the truth, but not so much of it that I gave something away. After all, the murderer could have been standing right there among us for all I knew.

"I was working with the police to help locate Wendy," I began. "Everybody felt she might know something about Tamara and who was responsible. We never expected to find her dead."

"Where did you find her?" asked Daria, uttering her first words of the day, at least to me.

I paused. "I can't really say."

Joel looked up from Chloe's phone. "It says she was in Laurel Canyon."

"That's right," I confirmed, bobbing my head.

"Was she hiking?" asked Heidi. Travis shushed her discreetly.

"What do you think?" said Chloe with a spiteful look. "It says she was shot in the chest. This wasn't a boulder."

"What the hell was she doing in Laurel Canyon?" asked Palmer.

I felt boxed in. People were beginning to ask me things I either didn't know or didn't want to talk about. Once again, totally by mistake, I was moving into the eye of the hurricane.

"I can't say anything right now."

Smack! The sound of a slap echoed through the morning air. I turned to see Laci standing in front of Rita, her hand still in the air.

"Stay away," she hissed.

Rita rubbed the side of her face, tears welling in her eyes. She seemed to crumple in front of all of us.

Beverly rushed over to her.

"What the hell was that about?" Travis asked.

"I have no idea," I replied.

Joel looked over at me grimly as he grabbed Chloe's hand. "We're getting out of here. This hasn't been a good morning."

That was certainly an understatement.

12

Travis and Heidi dropped me off at my place around noon. I was happy to find Madison in the study, working away. Even with the writing break I was taking, there was the website, correspondence and a bunch of other things to take care of.

"How was the funeral?" she asked.

"This isn't for *TMZ*, is it?" I couldn't help it. All the attention was making me paranoid.

"No way. I'm just curious. As a matter of fact, you've been pulled off the board as an assignment. Word is the police contacted management about the stakeout. Do you have connections?"

I thought about Detective Stefano and our motorcycle ride out to Malibu. "I don't know yet," I replied. "I'm working on it."

"Max told me to tell you he's going to be surfing at Zuma with friends. He'll be gone most of the afternoon."

"Gotcha," I said. "The funeral was nice, except when everybody heard about Wendy Strasser."

Madison's eyes grew wide. "I know. I heard about it at work. They think it might be a serial killer, someone stalking all the trophy wives of Beverly Hills."

"Oh, I don't know," I sighed, plopping down in my chair behind the desk. "I think serial killers have more important people to kill than trophy wives."

"Are you frightened?" asked Madison. "Living here, all alone."

"No," I said firmly. "I'm not sure why not, but I'm not. Maybe it's because I think Tamara's death and Wendy's death are connected. I don't know how, but I just think they are."

She gave me a shy glance. "You may get some help with that. Very soon."

"How so?"

"Detective Stefano called right before you got here. He's coming over at one to get a statement from you about Wendy Strasser's death. I told him you'd probably be here."

So we were going to see each other again. Somehow I felt that this couldn't be a bad thing.

"Sorry if I messed up your lunch," continued Madison.

"Messed it up? No, you didn't do that all." Before this I was going to eat cottage cheese out of the fridge; now things were looking considerably better. I dug into my purse, pulled out my credit card, and handed it to Madison. "Here, call Mr. Chow's and have them deliver some Chinese. For two. You know what I like. And then treat yourself to some lunch. Go to the Polo Lounge, you can put it on my tab."

"You're kidding!" she exclaimed.

"Not at all," I said. "Treat yourself. In fact, take a friend. You've earned it. I just think it might be more productive if I met Detective Stefano alone. We have things to talk about."

* * * *

"And you didn't see her again after that lunch at Barneys?" asked the Detective.

"Not until we found her body in Laurel Canyon," I replied. The white cardboard containers of Kung Pao chicken and broccoli and beef sat on the coffee table half finished; we hadn't gotten to the fortune cookies yet. I'd given the detective my statement, really just a corroboration of his, about finding Wendy's body in the garage apartment. Now it was time for some Q and A.

"Do you think they were killed the same day?" I asked.

"Looks that way. Certainly smelled that way from the waste that was present, the decomposition of the body. But we'll need the coroner to confirm that."

"When will that be?"

"Could be tomorrow, the next day. Bodies get backed up at the morgue just like planes at LAX."

"And 'til then?

He picked up the chopsticks and began to nibble on the broccoli and beef. "'til then I ask questions. That's my job."

"Who have you been asking, besides me?" If I wasn't a suspect – and I had to believe I wasn't—I wanted to know who was.

"The usual suspect is the husband. Or in this case, the ex-husband."

"You mean Joel and Lev Strasser?"

"Yeah, but the problem is, they might kill their own wives, but why would they kill the other guy's wife? Plus, they both have alibis for the mornings the murders occurred. Osmond was on the golf course at Hillcrest and Strasser was in a meeting with his senior staff."

"How did Lev take it when he learned Wendy had been murdered?"

"Pretty much went into shock. He cancelled all his appointments and went home for the day."

"If Lev stopped doing business, he must have really been upset. He never lets anything get in the way of that."

It was my turn to nibble on the Kung Pao Chicken. What can I tell you, I can't get enough of the peanuts. "So you think one person committed both murders?"

"It's likely. The weapon appears to have been the same in both killings. Of course, whoever killed them would have had to go from one location to the other."

"What about that nasty old landlady back in Laurel Canyon? Did she see anyone going into the apartment?"

He shook his head. "Annie Oakley? No, she was visiting her daughter in Santa Barbara up until yesterday."

"That's convenient."

"You told me Tamara gave you a book she wrote. Got a copy of it?"

"It wasn't her, it was her husband, Joel, who gave it to me. Hold on, I'll get it for you." I padded into the study, grabbed the manuscript and brought it back to him. "It's a Hollywood novel, lots of sex, lots of shopping."

He weighed it in his hand like it was a large melon he was contemplating buying at the supermarket. I wanted to warn him it was overripe. "Sounds like the kind of stuff you write."

"I like to think my books have a little more... zing."

He put the manuscript down on the coffee table. "I read one of them last night."

"Really? Which one?"

"*Hollywood Hills*, about the perfect young couple who break up when the husband falls for the co-star in his movie. Kind of reminded me of Brad and—"

"Detective," I said sharply, "all my books are fiction. Any resemblance to people living or dead is purely—"

He laughed. "Calm down. I kind of liked it. Especially that scene with the two girls and the grapes."

"What appealed to you? All the food?"

He looked at the cartons in front of him and shrugged. "Hey, I eat whatever's put in front of me." Then he looked back at the manuscript. "You think I should read this?"

I settled back on the sofa and looked at him in his dark blue I'm-a-homicide-cop suit. His Adam's apple bulged against the tight collar of his shirt. God, he was handsome.

"I don't think you should read it if you want to read a good book. But it is about a young woman who screws her way to the top in Hollywood. There might be something there for you, something about the murders."

"Did Mrs. Osmond dislike any specific young women?"

"Well she wasn't crazy about her stepdaughter Chloe, I can tell you that. Nobody really is, for that matter."

"You're talking about Chloe Osmond who runs the boutique on Robertson?"

I nodded.

"We checked her out the day after the first murder. She has an alibi, so does her friend."

"Who's that?"

"Laci Stivers."

That oxygen thief. Involuntarily, I made a face.

"I could almost believe they did it together," I muttered.

"No, they had an alibi. Laci Stivers's boyfriend backed them up. Come here, I'll show you."

He leaned over to the laptop I keep on the end of the coffee table. It was on, I always leave it on, you never know when inspiration will strike. He brushed the keypad, typed in a URL and up came a webpage for Santorini Spa. Next to a rendering of a building on Rodeo Drive, not far from where the funeral had been, was a picture of a very hunky looking guy. It was Mr. Gorgeous, the stud muffin I had seen Laci Stivers with at the Ivy.

"I think Laci's dating him," I said, pointing to the picture on the screen.

"Apparently." He nodded. "In any case, he runs the Spa and Laci and Chloe Osmond had coffee with him there the morning of the murder. Several employees confirmed it." He closed the webpage.

"There are a bunch of loose ends in any crime," he continued, placing the manuscript next to him on the sofa and patting it. "Maybe this is one of them. Maybe it's nothing. Same thing for the suitcases we found at the crime scene yesterday. Headquarters is going through them right now. We'll see."

"Well I think the manuscript will stink a lot more than the suitcases, even if they're stuffed with dirty laundry."

The Detective shot me a smile. "I gather you didn't like your friend's book?"

I let out a sigh. "I just get grumpy with all these trophy wives thinking they can sit down, vomit out a book in a couple of months at the computer and then be considered an author. Most of them are only being published because they're married to well connected, powerful men. It's like the movie stars who talk to a writer for about a week and then go out on tour with the autobiography they've 'written.'" I wiggled my fingers in the air over that verb.

"So the trophy wives just want what the movie stars have, a free ride? Isn't that what Hollywood is all about? Getting as much as you can while doing as little as possible?"

"Pretty much," I admitted. "It's the celebrity thing that drives it all. And now, after the stars have written their autobiographies, they start writing children's books. Like that takes a lot of effort. Dredging up some story your Mexican nanny told you and then the publishing house hires a great artist to illustrate it. They only publish those children's books because the stars can get booked on the talk shows and sell them. No other reason. I mean, I love Jamie Lee Curtis, we used to run into each other at a lot at parties way back when, but she should be ashamed."

His smile grew broader. "It's good yogurt, though."

"Yes," I laughed. "It is, and I like her, but come on, she's not a real writer."

"I read that Tori Spelling is writing a children's book."

"No!" It was a shock almost as deep and awful as the two corpses I'd unearthed.

"That's what I read."

"Oh my God! This is the end! She's writing a children's book? Why doesn't she just hike up her skirt and take a piss on Dr. Seuss's grave?"

He laughed out loud. "You're not a fan."

"Tori is to celebrity what Hitler was to political power: the abyss, a black hole." I had to be firm about this one.

"You told me you were an actress. You must have wanted to be a celebrity too."

I was exasperated enough to dive back into the remains of the Kung Pao. "Sure," I said. "Everybody does when they're a kid. But you grow up. And besides, no one could have become a celebrity off the movies I made in the eighties."

"They were cult movies?" he asked.

"Yes." I grinned. "Sadly, many of the people who went to see them later joined cults." I gulped down another mouthful of the sinful chicken. It was giving me energy and just tasted so damned good.

"Now that I've read one of your books, I guess I'll have to go out and rent one of your movies." He returned my grin.

"I'd like to rent one of yours," I replied, "if you'd only tell me the title of one of them."

He dismissed the idea with a wave of his hand. "Like I said before, it's a long story."

"Ah, Detective, you are so mysterious."

He reached over and placed his hand on mine. Just like that. "Why don't you call me Rocco," he said.

"Well, okay, Rocco."

"Or even Roc. That's what my friends call me." He took his hand away and smiled at me. He was going to have crows' feet someday, like I cared.

"Not too forward, I hope," he said softly.

"No, oh no," I said. And then I did something I hate myself for doing, but, damn it, I still did it. He was somewhere in his mid-thirties and I was... well I knew where I was. Which made me older than him. Made me a cougar, if you want to use that disgusting term. I don't use it because it sounds predatory, and I don't think an older woman being interested in a younger man is predatory. It's just common sense. Besides, cougar is a term men came up with, and I don't know about you, but I'm through with letting men define who I am. I'll define myself, thank you very much.

Still I'd be lying if I said I wasn't self-conscious about being with a younger man. We're all self-conscious when we're getting to know someone, and having him be younger ups the stakes tremendously. So, jerk that I am, I felt I had to say something about the age difference.

"I've been, you know, I've been around the block, as they say."

Rocco leaned forward and took my chin in his hand. "Hey, don't worry. I know that block. I used to live on that block."

"Really?"

"My last girlfriend was ten years older than me. This is not a new block."

"Welcome back to the neighborhood," I said as he leaned in and kissed me.

At first he pressed his lips on mine, but then his tongue came forward and I felt it enter my mouth as he reached behind me, grabbed my

91

shoulder and pulled me towards him, driving his tongue deeper so that I could feel and taste....

Which is why I didn't hear the door slam when Max came back from surfing.

When I saw him out of the corner of my eye, I leapt back on the sofa and tried to rearrange myself. Rocco held still, as I guess he'd learned to do at the scene of many a crime.

"Max, I didn't hear you. Did you have a good time surfing?"

He looked at me with a mixture of amusement, amazement, and just a pinch of distaste. "Yeah."

"Detective Stefano here was just asking me some questions. About the murders."

"Yeah."

"If, uh, you can wait a bit, maybe I can make some meatballs to go with that lasagna I made you last night."

"Whatever." And he was gone, up the stairs, into his room. But not out of my life. Never out of my life.

Rocco grabbed Tamara's manuscript and stood up. "I should probably go."

"Of course." I walked him to the door.

"Will you be okay?' he asked.

"Fine," I murmured, trying to process what had just happened. "I have to make him some dinner. Do his laundry too."

"I'll talk to you soon." He bent over and kissed me, then let himself out. I leaned back against the door, figuring out my next move.

Busted by my nineteen year old son as I was making out with a younger cop. Sooooo embarrassing.

13

I was on the second load of Max's laundry—the underwear and the sheets so gray, tattered, and wrinkled that they almost qualified as medieval tapestries—when Madison came back from lunch. The meatballs were sautéing in the kitchen. I was doing my best to get it all back to normal.

"Thanks so much for the treat," she said. "I took my friend Jenna. She'd never been to the Polo Lounge."

"You had fun?" I asked as I poked at the meatballs, throwing in some more garlic. Maybe that would make Max more forgiving.

"Oh yeah," replied Madison. "And guess who walked in while we were there? Laci Stivers and Chloe. Laci's boyfriend was with them."

"That hunky guy who owns the health spa?" Now I was interested.

Madison nodded. "Stavos Nikros, he's been with everybody. Though lately he's pretty much only been with Laci."

I lowered the flame on the meatballs. They weren't going anywhere. "What can you tell me about him?"

"Anything you want." She shrugged. "He's one of those club guys who's all over *TMZ*. Wanna see?"

I followed Madison over to the computer on the coffee table. She went to the *TMZ* website, typed in her ID, and went to the files section that was open only to employees. Two clicks on the touchpad and she was scrolling down the file labeled "Nikros, Stavos."

And there they were: Paris Hilton, Nicole Richie, Britney Spears, Gisele Bundchen, Kate Hudson, Anne Hathaway, and so many others. They were at a club, or an opening, or a fashion show, or a restaurant, and they were with Stavos. He either had his arm thrown around them, the way he'd done with Laci the other day at the Ivy, or he was kissing them, sometimes on the cheek (Anne Hathaway), sometime on the mouth (Nicole Richie). And they all looked so happy to be with him.

"What is this guy on? A testosterone drip?"

"He started out as a masseur, believe it or not. Women were practically beating down the doors for his services."

I looked at his long, thick hands, wrapped around either a drink or a woman's waist in picture after picture. "Magic fingers, huh?"

Madison nodded. "Eventually he was so popular that, a few months ago, Laci Stivers is supposed to have given him a bunch of cash and he bought out the original owners. Now it's his place."

The pictures of Stavos and the women of Hollywood kept scrolling up. There was even one of him with Lindsay Lohan, their lips locked over a birthday cake ablaze with candles.

"Wow," I muttered, "looks like Stavos could change a girl's mind."

"That was before Sam." Madison clicked over to his personal information page. The endless crawl of Stavos with all those adoring women reminded me of something my dad once said when he was Burt Reynolds's stunt double back in the seventies. "Burt was butter on a plate. All those ladies just kept landing on him like flies."

His personal information showed that Stavos was 29, six foot, two inches, 200 pounds, and of Greek descent but born in Des Moines, Iowa. He had moved to Hollywood "to become a rock star" —has anyone ever moved here to become a classical musician? —and "meet hot chicks." Clearly, he had already achieved one half of his life's ambitions.

"Look at this." Madison moved the cursor over to a section labeled Inspiration. It read "I live my life for God, because God is love. And I have found God in Luna."

"Luna again," I murmured. "That damn thing is popping up everywhere."

Madison nodded. "It's incredibly popular right now. The new Kabbalah."

"I even read that Palmer Collins joined it. And he's supposed to be a born again Christian, after that Jesus movie he made."

"Luna's totally non-denominational." Madison typed in a URL and brought up its webpage. "The idea is you can still be a Christian or a Jew and follow Luna at the same time."

"What's to follow?" I asked. "It's just the same kind of self-improvement cult that's been popular out here forever, like EST or Scientology. They just have better graphics to go with the internet. Aimee Semple McPherson never had a webpage."

"Try Facebook." Madison navigated over to Vance Packer's Facebook page. His round face, still boyish but fraying around the edges, smiled out over a message that said, "Luna is love."

"His tweets are more popular than Ashton Kushner's."

"He's a washed up singer from a busted boy band," I muttered. "Really, Madison, at the risk of sounding 107 instead of the mere slip of girl I still think I am, I just don't get it all. Twitter, Facebook, the internet, it's all so up to date, and yet what is everybody chasing? Inner peace. Vance Packer has just cooked up a new way to serve it, and dopes like

Laci Stivers and this guy Stavos and Palmer Collins are lining up for it like it's a twenty dollar hamburger. Compared to Luna, throwing the I Ching was a bit of brain surgery."

Madison smiled at another one of what we had decided to call my "old school rants." You know you're getting older when yesterday's stupidity seems better to you than today's stupidity.

"Those burgers cost more than twenty dollars," said Madison, going back to the Luna webpage. It detailed the way Vance's "religion" worked. You paid a thousand dollars to become a "Luna associate," which qualified you to go out in the world and sell memberships to other folks, or "Lunatics," as the media, quite accurately I felt, called them. Sell enough memberships and you graduated to "Luna manager," then "director," "commander," and on up the line to "astral visionary." Luna was just a Ponzi scheme selling inner peace. And, of course, you could get rich in the process. Making inner peace the product was the smart part: it was quite shrewd of Vance, since no one could bring the "product" to the Better Business Bureau and claim it was defective. Who wanted to be known as so dumb that you paid a thousand bucks to be happy? Vance had become a clever little ducky since the days he stuffed a sock in his crotch and crooned hits like "Lady, Be My Baby" with the rest of the boys in Playerz.

"I'm surprised a big ladies' man like Stavos fell for this," I said. "What's in it for him?"

"The thinking at *TMZ* is that it must have something to do with Laci," said Madison. "She's been his ticket in to a lot of big things, as well as backing his spa. And he's supposed to be very ambitious, wants to be a player. So I would bet he's following her lead."

"Why would *she* be attracted to Luna? She's already got all the money in the world." Common sense, you can't beat it.

"She's always chasing after the latest thing, at least for the publicity. And besides, she and Vance went to high school together, Crossroads in Santa Monica."

"They were involved?"

"Just friends I think," said Madison. "But real, deep down kind of friends." Shallow people being deep down, it was so L.A. "But she's been pretty much with Stavos for the past year, hot and heavy."

"And he keeps her that happy?" I asked as I looked again at his *TMZ* page which Madison had surfed back to. He was damned good looking, but then, out here, who isn't?

95

"Apparently. That's his strong suit, anyway. There are supposed to be lots of broken hearts all over town."

I thought back to Laci slapping Rita Collins at Tamara's funeral this morning. No reason why Rita couldn't be one of those broken hearts. Especially with what Beverly had told me at Hilda Mazur's, about Rita's hush-hush love affair.

"There's a Luna benefit tonight that Laci and Stavos are hosting," added Madison. She found the listing on the *TMZ* assignment page. "They're having a fund raiser at No Exit on Sunset, Vance Packer is co-hosting." No Exit was the latest in a string of "you-can't-get-in-here-unless-you're-twenty-anorexic-and-famous" joints that spring up on Sunset Boulevard like weeds. They last about a year apiece and then go back to being Mail Boxes Are Us or 7-11s.

Madison clicked off the *TMZ* webpage and brought the computer back to my homepage. "You know, Madison," I said as we strolled back to the kitchen, "you ought to take notes on all of this. There's a book in it for you."

"Oh I don't know,' she sighed. "Brett Easton Ellis has probably already written that book."

But it wasn't Brett Easton Ellis we found nibbling on the meatballs, it was Max.

"Hungry?" I said, seeing him for the first time since he had caught me necking in Lover's Lane.

"I guess," he shrugged. "Just looking for something to eat."

"Sit down. I'll fix you a plate." Supper therapy is a great thing; it's saved a lot of us mothers in a pinch. "Madison, do you want to join us?"

She shook her head. "I'm going to hop, if that's okay with you."

"Sure sweetie, I'll see you tomorrow." I microwaved a slab of lasagna, then piled some meatballs on top of it and set it in front of Max. I wasn't hungry for a full dinner myself, so I scarfed down a Little Debbie Cake as I prepared his meal.

He said nothing, just grabbed a fork and began whittling away. And he wasn't looking at me either.

"You like the meatballs?" I asked.

He shrugged again and kept eating.

"I spent an hour making them."

"They're fine." He speared another one and made it disappear in a single gulp.

"I'm glad you like them. I can make more if you want. You can bring them back to the dorm, share them with your friends."

"That's okay."

"It's no problem, really. I have some more ground sirloin and I've got boxes and boxes of bread crumbs left over from when I was feeding that flock of doves that nested in the tree in the front...."

Max dropped his fork on the counter. "So how come you were making it with that dude when I came in?"

"I was not 'making it' with him!" I protested. "We shared... a kiss. That's all."

"Well, it was kinda gross to see your Mom making out with some random dude in the living room, you know? I mean, it's cool and all, but get a room, huh?"

"Get a room? I have a room!" I raised my arms and swept them around the kitchen. "I have a whole house. You're the one with a room. And it's in this house!"

"It doesn't bother me, Mom. I just didn't know anything about this guy. The way it happened, it was all so random. That's all." He was calmer than me about the whole thing, but then, he didn't have anything to be embarrassed about.

"We're just getting to know each other, that's all." I picked up a spoon, reached into the pan and piled some more meatballs on his plate. "You're okay with this?"

"No big deal." He flashed me a smile. I love it when my kid smiles.

"Good," I replied. "Then maybe you can help me with something."

"Like what?"

"I need someone to take me to a benefit at No Exit tonight. And Max, my son, it looks like you've been elected."

14

For the first two years of our marriage Travis and I lived up in the Hollywood Hills in a sprawling ranch house that we dubbed Rehab Central. Most of the band members used to crash there between marriages or girlfriends. It was a rustic place, backed right up against a hill overgrown with gnarled, old trees and dense, clinging vines. And somewhere up on that hill lived a lone coyote that came down every so often to hunt and kill our cats or the neighbors' dogs. I grew to hate that mean, mangy animal.

But no matter what we did, traps, fences, sound devices, we couldn't get rid of the coyote. One morning I dropped a skillet full of scrambled eggs on my foot when I looked out the kitchen window and saw him sitting in the middle of the backyard, right next to the crib we had put out there for Max. I began to cry, but by the time Travis got to me the coyote was gone. That's when he went into the garage and got his rifle. I cleaned up the mess on the floor, bandaged my foot and made another batch of eggs. Travis disappeared up the hill. About twenty minutes later, I heard a single shot.

When he came back to the house Travis looked at me and said, "Sometimes you have to go where a thing lives to kill it."

This was my thinking about going to Laci Stivers' Luna benefit at No Exit. I needed to hunt her down in her own environment. There was a problem, however. Max thought I was out of my mind.

"You're giving tongue to a cop in the living room and now you want me to take you out on a date? Mom, this is seriously too weird for me!"

"I'm asking you to accompany me on a fact finding mission," I said as I cleared away his plate and put the meatballs in the refrigerator. "One that's going to take you to one of the hottest clubs in L.A. Now all we have to do is figure out a way to get in."

"Taking my mom to a club? This is a reality show. We'll wind up on You Tube!"

"It's going to be fun," I insisted.

"It's going to be child abuse," he replied.

"Do you love me?"

"Of course."

"Well then if you love me, you'll be my escort to No Exit tonight. I need to get to Laci Stivers and this is the only way I know how to do it."

"No way." He crossed his arms over his chest and leaned back in his chair.

"Max, you don't understand. There have been two murders. It looks like I'm involved, at least to some people. And there was an incident at Tamara's funeral that makes me think that Laci Stivers knows something about all this."

He hadn't moved from his crossed-arms position, so I reached for some heavy artillery. "Besides, you wouldn't want me to tell your Dad I've changed my mind about him giving you money for Hawaii."

"That's blackmail, Mom," he said.

I shook my head. "No, it's not. It's real life. You scratch my back, I'll scratch yours."

"There is no way I am taking you to No Exit. One of my fraternity brothers works the front door."

"Perfect! Now we have a way to get in."

Max stood up; he wanted to leave the room. "Mom, people are going to think I'm some sort of weird perv. I can't take you out to a club and have my fraternity brother and other people see me with you."

"Oh don't worry, dear. I'm going to be in disguise."

* * * *

Two hours later I came downstairs in a black Goth gown that had been in the back of my closet for close to two decades. To accessorize it I wore a silver cross necklace and a silk shawl draped over my shoulders. And I had found a stringy blond wig I'd worn to a Halloween party at David Lee Roth's more years ago than I cared to remember. I thought that the wig, plus my sunglasses, would hide my age, give me a nice, eccentric edge, and make me absolutely unidentifiable.

"How do I look?" I said to Max, turning around and modeling my outfit.

"Like that woman that Dad used to date before he met you," he replied, stifling a yawn.

"Pat Benatar? But she's not a blond."

"Not her," he replied. "The one who whirls around like a top."

"Stevie Nicks? From Fleetwood Mac?"

Max nodded. "Well that's good, that'll throw them off. Now what about drugs?"

"What about them, Mom? You know I don't do them."

"Of course I know that. But what about Laci? Don't you think she does them?"

"You think people act that way normally?"

"Exactly! So I think I need to have something with me, some kind of drug or something that makes me look hip, like I'm part of her scene. What are the kids at school into?"

"Like you've never done drugs, Mom?"

This is a conversation any parent has to have with their child, but it's a hard one if you were married to a rock star. When Max turned twelve Travis and I sat down with him, told him that no wise child repeats the mistakes of his parents, and both admitted to having smoked pot. Which was true, but in Travis' case, not the entire truth. After we split up, I never asked him if he had opened up the conversation again with Max. One of the things I've found to be true as a parent is that if it's not a problem, you don't bring it up. There are enough things to deal with that you don't have to go hunting for a crisis. And, thankfully, drugs hadn't been a problem with Max; the things he chose to abuse were cell phones and video games.

"Well, Max, I've been around rock and roll for more than twenty years. I've smoked the odd joint."

"Mom, I know that you and Dad used to do weed. You told me. It's cool. It's that whole Woodstock thing."

"Woodstock! I wasn't at Woodstock!" I shrieked. "I was a baby then. I was practically in diapers.'

"So were most of those hippie dudes that were high on all that weed," he replied with a laugh.

Inspiration finally struck. "I know, I'll bring some baby powder and pass it off as cocaine. Your Dad used to do that with some of the band members when they were trying to kick the stuff."

"You're going to be snorting baby powder with Laci Stivers?" he asked.

"Why not?" I replied. "She's only got the mind of a little child to begin with." By the time we left I had a perfect silver foil package of baby powder stowed in my purse along with my lipstick, eyeshadow and loose change. On the way out I grabbed another Little Debbie Cake and stuffed it into the purse as well. For energy, right?

* * * *

Half a century ago, the Sunset Strip was home to the most glamorous nightclubs in this city. Gorgeous movie stars such as Lana Turner, Ava Gardner, and Rita Hayworth used to get dressed up in furs and diamonds to dance at swank supper clubs with exotic names like The Tropicana or

The Macombo. Now nymphets-du-jour like Kim Kardashian, Lindsay Lohan, Britney Spears and Laci Stivers flash their crotches as they jump out of their SUVs, run the gauntlet of the paparazzi, and spend the night at an overpriced dump like No Exit. To my mind, this is not progress.

Max pulled my Bentley up to the valet at No Exit, handed him the keys and said to me, "For this, you have to tell Dad I get to rent a boat for a day in Hawaii, a cabin cruiser."

"Done," I replied as we walked up to the entrance of the club. Max greeted his bouncer pal at the door and they had a quick chat. The pal then turned to the head bouncer, a thick, thuggish looking Italian with a network of gold chains hanging around his neck. Mr. Meatball, as I decided to nickname him later when I learned his other profession, looked me up and down like discounted merchandise at Wal-Mart. Then he beckoned me forward and stared past my sunglasses into my eyes.

"Am I supposed to know you?" he asked. He was waving his fingers right below my chin as he spoke. The scent of garlic rose from his knuckles like fetid perfume.

"I don't know," I replied. "Are you from Bayonne?"

"I once ate a pizza there," he deadpanned.

"Yeah. Great pizza."

He smiled. "Yeah, it is great." He nodded to Max's pal and said, "They're in."

We practically jumped through the front door. As we did I heard Max's bouncer pal whisper to him, "Dude, I didn't know you were into cougars."

"A yacht," muttered Max, "I get a yacht for doing this for you."

We walked down a corridor and into a narrow room whose walls had been painted a warm chocolate, the color of freshly made pudding. Those walls had then been covered with vintage Playmate of the Month centerfolds, each one in a gilt frame. Instead of seats, naugahyde sofas in varying shades of lime and orange were grouped all over the room. Crystal martini glasses stood in formation on the bar, next to polished cocktail shakers. And over to the side, sitting on its own boomerang-shaped coffee table, was an old stereo, or hi-fi as my parents used to say. The record mounted on its spindle dropped down to the turntable, the playing arm automatically descended on it, and the cool, lush tones of Julie London crooning *Cry Me A River* filled the room. The place was a swinging 60s bachelor's pad, as reimagined by some a clever designer who been watching too many episodes of *Mad Men*.

101

And completing the illusion was Hugh Hefner, who sat on one of the lime sofas, surrounded by three young women whose breasts were being squeezed out of the tops of their gowns like toothpaste from a tube. People kept coming over to Hef, shaking his hand and having their picture taken with him. I've always liked him, and thought that his take on sex was spot on, but really, to be in your eighties and sitting at a club full of young, sexed-up kids? I mean, what were the girls going to give him when they got home to the Mansion, a hand job or a heart massage?

"This is fantastic," I said to Max as we sat down on one of the sofas.

"This is humiliating," he shot back. The coffee table in front of us had a 50s style red plastic Mr. Peanut bowl on it, filled to the brim with fresh peanuts. I swooped down and grabbed a handful.

"Can I get you folks something to drink?" asked a svelte young waitress with a Jetson's hairdo and huge, blue plastic globe earrings that kept blinking on and off.

"A diet coke," I said.

"Red Bull," grumbled Max.

She skittered off to the bar, and I turned to the entrance and saw a large balloon head bobbing on a stick body, like those drawings of missing children that they used to put on milk cartons. It was Mary Kate Olson, or Ashley Olson, I could never be bothered to tell them apart on that sitcom they did, *Full House*, or *Empty Nest*, or *Half Baked*, whatever the hell it was called. She was plastered into one of those red leather John Paul Gautier outfits that make us normal sized women shudder. But she looked lovely and smiled at everyone as she traipsed across the room carrying a huge, black Marc Jacobs handbag that looked like it weighed more than she did.

"Cool. Mary Kate," said Max, who liked to watch corny, old sitcoms on You Tube.

"Are you sure?" I asked. "What if it's the other one?"

"Mom, I've been hot for her since I was like seven."

Mary Kate shifted her enormous bag from one shoulder to the other as she passed us and almost capsized. As she did, it was possible, momentarily, to see her for what she really was, a tiny skiff adrift on the turbulent winds of celebrity. A credit card fell out of her bag; I reached down and picked it up. "You're right, it is Mary Kate. We should give this to her." She had already disappeared into the crowd at the bar.

I was about to stand up and seek her out when our waitress returned. "Diet Coke and a Red Bull," she said, setting our drinks down on the table. "That'll be fifty two dollars please."

"Fifty two dollars!" I exclaimed. "We ordered a Coke and an energy drink, not dinner for twelve."

She smiled sweetly as her earrings kept blinking on and off. "The Diet Coke is fifteen dollars and the Red Bull is twenty."

"You're only up to thirty five," I countered.

"The club adds on a seventeen dollar charge. That brings it to fifty two."

"A seventeen dollar charge? For what?" I couldn't get over these prices.

"It's an entertainment charge," she replied.

I gestured down to the coffee table in front of us. "When do the peanuts start dancing?"

Her stony face told me that I was not the first customer to blanch at these ridiculous prices. "I could swipe your credit card if you like."

I handed over Mary Kate's American Express card which was still in my hand. "Swipe away," I replied.

"Mom, you're a criminal," protested Max.

"No, I'm not," I snapped. "I'm just sensible. Now let's take these drinks and move before she comes back." We faded into a crowd gathered in the Kon Tiki corner, which was nothing more than a feeble grass hut and a few coconut shells. People were jostling us left and right; I began to feel like Max and I had washed up on Gilligan's Island. Maybe this wasn't such a good idea after all.

"Where's Laci Stivers?" I grumbled to Max.

"Over there." He pointed to a roped off area behind the bar. She was wearing a silver-sequined minidress and her eyes were outlined in huge circles of black mascara. It gave her a kind of Edie Sedgewick look that was not out of place in the club. Sitting on either side of her were Stavos and Vance Packer. Vance was stuffed into a white dress shirt and a dinner jacket like a pimento stuck in an olive, definitely not his look. But Stavos was all easy charm, his chest pressing against a black silk shirt that was half open. Between the two of them, Laci, so tiny and bony, looked like an aspiring human sacrifice. But this odd trio seemed to be having a great time, holding half full martini glasses and laughing together, as if they were playing a private joke on the rest of us.

More surprising than that, though, was the presence of Palmer Collins and his new wife, Daria, who sat with the three of them. Like Hef, Palmer was well past his sell by date in this crowd.

"What is Palmer Collins doing here?" I hissed to Max, lifting my sunglasses and jerking them in that direction.

"You're asking me?" said Max. He took a swig of his drink. "And by the way, this Red Bull is warm."

"What do you want for twenty dollars?" I chuckled.

Then a publicist came over to the group and pulled Vance aside. She handed him some notes and a hand microphone, and he strutted out to the center of the floor as the club's music system was turned off. Palmer and Daria moved with him, while Laci and Stavos stayed on the sidelines.

"First of all, I want to thank you for being here, tonight," Vance began. "We all love to party, but when you party with a purpose, you're really doing God's work. And that's what Luna is all about."

Applause, led by Daria, broke out from the crowd. Those martinis people were drinking must have been very strong.

Vance looked around the room and saw everyone focused on him, further proof that his original boy band stardom hadn't really left him, although Hef had fallen asleep on the bosom of one of his escorts. "As you know, Luna is less than five years old," he continued, "so the awesome growth that we have recently experienced has been so amazing. We've just opened a headquarters in San Diego and have plans to open one in New York next year."

"Big whoop!" cheered Daria raising her fist, Palmer by her side. She was about as convincing a cheerleader as she'd been a Virgin Mary.

"Tonight is special to us because it's the kickoff to a week of benefits for Luna," continued Vance. "We're working to defray the cost of some of the overages for converting a vacant building on Hollywood Boulevard to The Collins Center, our new headquarters. We've taken an old twelve story high rise, gutted it from top to bottom, and put in the latest technology. The Collins Center is going to be the epicenter of the Luna revolution!"

"Yay, Palmer Collins!" cheered Daria. He nodded and waved to the crowd, giving them his best action star noblesse oblige.

What the hell does Palmer Collins have to do with all this? I thought to myself. But I didn't need to ask because Vance had the answer to my question.

"By donating some of the profits he made from his awesome birth of Jesus flick, *Thunder Over Bethlehem*, Palmer has helped us obtain the lease and do the renovations on the Collins Center," he continued to more applause. "In fact, Palmer has even generously gotten Zenith Studios to donate some of the proceeds from the premiere of his new animated film, *Fool's Goldfish*, to keep the Collins Center up and running for the first year of its existence."

This brought more cheers from Daria, more phony grins from Palmer. I grabbed my cell phone and sent myself a reminder text about "Fool's Goldfish." I had a connection for the premiere of that film, and now I wanted to use it.

"So let's have a big hand for Palmer Collins!" concluded Vance.

As Palmer walked to the center of the room, I looked over and saw Laci whispering in Stavos' ear. He nodded and she walked off to the ladies' room.

"This is my cue," I said to Max. I followed her, threading my way through the crowd, a mix of starving starlets, gay agents, and personal trainers with multi-colored tattoos crawling up their arms like large insects. As the door to the ladies' room closed behind me, I heard Palmer say, "I know it's unusual for an actor to be humble, but tonight..."

Laci was by herself, staring into the mirror and reapplying her eyeliner. I stood next to her and pulled a lipstick out of my purse.

"You look great tonight," I said to her.

"Thanks," she replied without even looking at me.

"All that black eyeshadow," I continued. "It really gives you an Edie Segewick look."

"Thanks."

The compliments weren't working, so I decided to play a higher card. I reached into my purse again, this time pulling out the foil packet of baby powder I'd made up back at my place. I unfolded it and put it on the sink counter we were sharing.

"Like to do a line?" I asked her, offering her a small straw.

"Oh sure," gushed Laci. Now we were pals. She leaned down and snorted up a thick line of the filmy white baby powder. A moment later she was coughing like she'd been caught in a desert sand storm.

"Aren't you doing any?" she asked, handing me back the straw.

"I did some during Vance Packer's speech," I replied.

"Oh well." She took the straw and did another line. "What did you say your name was?"

I looked over at my purse. "I didn't. I'm Debbie, Debbie Cakes," I said. "I was Tamara Osmond's nutritionist. I saw you yesterday at her funeral." I extended my hand and Laci shook it. Her utterly blank look told me that my disguise was working.

"Wasn't that so weird?" she replied. "One moment she's alive and the next, she's, like, dead. Makes you think."

"Oh yeah." I nodded my head in sympathy. "Were you very close to Tamara?"

"Not really. I was there because I'm a friend of her step-daughter, Chloe Osmond."

"Oh," I exclaimed wide-eyed. "You mean the Chloe Osmond who runs Chlothes on Robertson?" I was doing my best Little Bo Peep for Laci, hoping she wouldn't see through it.

She pulled out her lipstick and reapplied it, studying her reflection in the mirror, as if it contained the secret of human existence, rather than a lot of cell phone chatter and the latest tweets from Perez Hilton. "She's supposed to be meeting us here," Laci whined. "I don't know what's keeping her. Chloe is, like, always late."

"Some people are just that way," I cooed sympathetically. "Take Rita Collins, another client of mine. She's always late."

Laci eyes flashed with just the barest hint of interest. "Rita Collins is a client of yours?"

"Yes," I lied. "She's a vegetarian, so I've been creating a new diet for her."

"She doesn't look as if she's had any meat in her mouth for a long time," laughed Laci. "Maybe she'd be better off blowing a carrot after all."

"I gather you don't like her."

"Why do you say that?"

"Well, I saw you slap her yesterday at Tamara's funeral."

Laci raised her hand and whished it through the air in a slapping motion. "Aerobics," she giggled. Then her smile disappeared. "She's just a big nothing, and she bothers me."

"Oh yeah." I dropped my foil packet back in my purse, next to the Little Debbie Cake. "I've found her to be a very demanding client. What's your beef with her?"

"That she's alive," she replied enigmatically. And then she pulled her sunglasses out of her purse and slipped them on. In the brightly lit ladies room mirror, glammed to the hilt and both in our dark glasses, we looked like a pair of designer robots.

Laci rubbed her nose. "You know, that stuff you gave me isn't doing anything."

"It comes on real slow," I said. "But you'll love the high. It's as soft as a baby's bottom."

"Take care, Debbie," said Laci as she pushed the door open and walked back into the club. I followed her, but had to stop dead in my tracks as the door closed behind me. Our Jetsons waitress was staring at me, her earrings blinking on and off furiously. She held the credit card I had given her in her hand.

"When did you become Mary Kate Olson?" she demanded.

Figuring that outraged virtue might be the best way out of this, I grabbed the card and said, "Let me see that!" The waitress reached for it back when—

Pop! Pop! Pop!

Three loud gunshots went off in a row. Everyone froze for a second, and then a girl began to scream. "Don't shoot us! Don't shoot us!"

The crowd cleared the middle of the room in a small stampede.

Chloe was struggling with the huge bouncer, Mr. Meatball, who had a gun in his hand. She had wrapped her hand around the barrel of the gun and they were fighting for possession of it. Small as she was, she had managed to pin her legs around Mr. Meatballs's waist and was digging into him with her stilettos as she wrestled for the weapon.

"Don't shoot us!" the girl kept screaming.

Like a drunken couple in a dance marathon, Chloe and Mr. Meatball swayed across the club floor as people ducked under tables and sofas.

Pop!

Another shot rang from the gun. Now panic was setting in; the agents were beginning to scream.

I caught Max's eye and pointed to the back exit. We both dashed towards it while the rest of the crowd headed for the front entrance.

Max pulled the door open, we barreled through it and collapsed into the club's back alley.

"Get the car now!" I panted. "We've got to get the hell out of here."

He vaulted down the alley as the exit door flew open again. Palmer and Daria burst through it, his iPhone was pressed to his ear.

"They're shooting people in there!" he exclaimed. "Meet me in the back alley. We'll wait for you here." He gave Daria a hug. "We'll find them."

"We should never leave them in the car again," said Daria.

"Are you okay?" I asked. They looked over at me, not even a flicker of recognition on their faces, thanks to the wig and dark glasses.

"We're fine," replied Palamer. "Thanks for asking."

"We shouldn't have left them in the car," repeated Daria.

"Your keys?" I said.

She shook her head. "Our bodyguards. We let them sit in the car instead of coming in with us." She shot Palmer a look. "This was supposed to be a charity event, something safe. Who says you can trust Luna?"

"You can trust Luna," he said in a tone that indicated this conversation was over.

"Is everybody okay back there?" I asked.

"I think so," said Palmer. "The other bouncers pulled the two of them apart and someone called the cops. I don't know what the hell's gotten into Chloe Osmond."

"Probably not too many drinks," I offered. "I mean, who could afford them?"

"I know," clucked Daria. "Don't you just hate that about this place? "

Palmer's phone rang and he put it back to her ear. "Oh hi, Johnny. No, I'm fine." He mouthed the words "Johnny Depp" to Daria. "Really, I am. I think it's all over now. But thanks for calling."

I gave them a wave and headed down the alley and around the corner, back to Sunset and the entrance of No Exit. As I did I saw a white KCLM news van pull up to the curb. Lisa Manning, in full blond mane, jumped out of it with a microphone poised in her hand like she was landing on Omaha Beach. Two of the bouncers had blocked the front entrance to the club, holding back the folks who were trying to get out. Lisa looked over at me and sprang into action.

Gesturing wildly to her crew, who ran behind her, she began speaking rapidly. "Lisa Manning for KCLM, and we're here at the site of tonight's shooting at the hip club No Exit. What was supposed to be a benefit for the Luna religion has turned into an evening of attempted murder on the Sunset Strip." She gestured "cut" by crossing her hand under chin. Then she wheeled around, walked over and thrust the microphone in my face.

"Did you see the shooting inside?" demanded Lisa. Her cameraman was so close to my face I could see a small hair growing out of the mole on his chin.

"Yes I did," I replied, "it was shocking. Just shocking."

"You have all the details?" she asked breathlessly.

"Every one," I replied nodding my head.

"And your name is?" demanded Lisa.

"Debbie Cakes," I replied. "Nutritionist to the stars."

The sound guy held up his wrist and tapped his watch. "It's eleven o'clock, Lisa. We're going live."

"Gotcha," she said. Then she grabbed my wrist in a death grip and said to me, "Don't move. We're going live on the air in twenty seconds."

Lisa pressed on her earpiece, shook her blond hair into the semblance of a hairdo and looked up straight at the cameraman.

"Yes Chuck, I can hear you," she said, "I'm here live at No Exit on the Sunset Strip where there has been a shooting incident inside the club. And I'm with an eyewitness, Debbie Cakes, the famous nutritionist to some of Hollywood's brightest stars. Hi Debbie."

"Hi Lisa." This was going to be fun.

"Please tell our viewers about the terrible shooting that just occurred on the floor of No Exit."

"Well," I said, taking a pause so I could draw the whole thing out, "someone had a gun in there and they just shot Tori Spelling."

"No!" exclaimed Lisa, her eyeballs morphing into two small planets, like the earrings that had been hanging from the waitress's ears just moments ago.

"Yes!" I exclaimed back. "But she's okay. They just shot her in the butt."

Lisa turned to the camera and intoned solemnly. "Chuck, we have just learned that in a tragic event here on the Sunset Strip Tori Spelling has been shot in the ass by an unknown assailant."

I grabbed the microphone from Lisa. "She's perfectly okay," I said. "They're just a bit worried that the bullet that went in her ass may have caused some brain damage."

I heard the squeal of some very expensive tires as Max pulled my Bentley up to curb. Lisa was petrified, not quite believing what I'd said. I tossed the microphone back to her.

"See you later," I said over my shoulder as I dodged into the car, and Max jammed his foot down on the gas pedal.

"I'm never taking you out again on a date, Mom," groused Max as the lights of the Strip sped by us and we charged back into Beverly Hills.

I pulled off my wig and dark glasses and threw them in the back seat. "You don't have to," I replied. "I've had enough fun for one night."

15

After my big night out I slept in until almost ten the next morning, then drifted down to the kitchen for some coffee. There was a note from Max on the counter: "Bye Mom, please try to be more appropriate in the future." I stirred two packets of Splenda into my cup of French Roast, picked up the remote, and turned on the television.

There on the screen was the video of my meeting with Lisa Manning last night. "Tori Spelling has been shot in the ass!" she blurted out, and then Lisa's audio dropped out as an announcer said, "Shocking developments in a Sunset Strip shooting, next on KCLM All Action Morning News."

I reached for last night's Little Debbie Cake, but it had melted into a chocolate soft sculpture in my purse. So I threw a bagel in the toaster oven and sat down to watch the news. Now everybody jokes about their local newscasters, but the folks who do it in Southern California, especially in the off hours, are a breed unto themselves. KCLM's morning new show was anchored by, I'm not kidding, Ken and Barbie. This being multi-cultural Southern California, however, Ken was Ken Park, a Korean, and Barbie was Barbie Sanchez, a Latina. He had jet black hair and piercing eyes; she had wavy brunette hair and false eyelashes so big they practically broke through the screen and brushed the back of your hand. They both looked great. Everybody on Southern California news looks great. Just don't ask them to add up the lunch check or find China on a map of the world.

"Breaking news about a shooting spree on the Sunset Strip," said Ken. "And here with exclusive video of it is our own Lisa Manning."

Lisa's huge blond head hovered into view like a praying mantis. "Thank you, Ken," she said. "KCLM was first on the scene with exclusive details of the incident at the trendy club No Exit last night."

"Shots were fired?" asked a wide-eyed Barbie.

"Yes they were, Barbie," replied Lisa. "Insiders tell us that a struggle occurred in the club between Chloe Osmond, the daughter of Hollywood producer Joel Osmond, and a security guard, Anthony Salazar. We have the video."

On the screen I saw Chloe and then Mr. Meatball being led out of the club by the police. Neither one was in handcuffs.

"Anyone arrested?" Ken asked Lisa.

"Anthony Salazar has been held overnight. Chloe Osmond was released and picked up by her father just an hour after the event."

"Nobody was hurt then?" said Barbie.

"No," replied Lisa darkly, "but that was not the big news of the evening. Prior to entering the club I spoke with a witness named Debbie Cakes who offered false information about the shooting."

There I was on the news in my wig and dark glasses. "Someone had a gun in there and they just shot Tori Spelling." There was an edit and then I was saying, "They just shot her in the butt."

"Oh my Lord!" exclaimed Barbie, as shocked as if she'd been told the President had just collapsed. "Is that true?"

"No, Barbie, it's not," said Lisa. "And I and the KCLM news team are determined to get to the bottom of this evil prank." Clearly Lisa had lost some points with her on-air newscast last night.

"We have a statement from Tori Spelling's management team," Lisa continued, reading from a document. "Tori Spelling was not shot in the buttocks last night at the No Exit club on the Sunset Strip. She was at home with her family, memorizing her lines for an upcoming production of *A Streetcar Named Desire* in which she is to play Blanche Du Bois. Ms. Spelling wishes to reassure her fans that she is fine and hopes to discover why KCL—"

Lisa dropped the paper. "As you can imagine, Barbie, she's terribly upset."

"Oh I can see why," she agreed. "Why would anybody want to spread such a vicious lie about Tori Spelling?"

Lisa pushed her profile forward as if she were the Statue of Liberty. "The answer lies with Debbie Cakes."

"What do we know about this Debbie Cakes?" said Ken.

"The KCLM team is on it as we speak," replied Lisa. "Apparently she is a nutritionist to the stars, fashioning eating plans for the rich and famous. For all we know, Ken, she may be spreading rumors, or tainted food, to the stars right this very second!"

Barbie shook her head and clucked sympathetically. "Upsetting news, Lisa. Thanks for keeping us updated. We'll hear more from you soon, I hope."

"Count on it, Barbie," replied Lisa, raising a clenched fist in her best crime fighter fashion.

I smelled the bagel just beginning to burn, so I snagged it from the toaster oven and spread some cream cheese on it, giggling all the while.

I'd gotten back at Lisa Manning for naming me as a suspect in Tamara's murder, and, really, who had I hurt with my little masquerade? I mean, what were they going to do, arrest me for impersonating a nutritionist?

An hour later I was in my Bentley heading towards Rodeo Drive and the Santorini Spa, where I had just made an appointment for a massage by Stavos Nikros. I wanted to see what all the talk was all about, what he was all about. And besides, I was sore as hell from running around like a teenager last night.

I speed dialed Travis on my cell phone.

"You're up early," he said.

"It's eleven o'clock," I protested.

"Well, early considering that you been out on the Strip drinking and shooting up night clubs."

"Max called you."

"Be careful of your son, Nikki. He may write a book about you someday."

"I need a favor, Travis."

"What would that be?"

I took a breath; this was going to be a biggie. "Remember how you told me you were working on a song for *Fool's Goldfish*, the new animated film from Zenith?"

"Course I do. I even sing it under the credits. The premiere's tonight at Graumann's Chinese."

"I want to go with you." I gulped.

There was a pause. "I usually go to these things with my wife," Travis finally replied.

"I used to be your wife," I countered.

"And when you were, we went to premieres together. Of your movies."

"So now I want to see one of yours," I said brightly.

There was another pause. "Actually, I've been wanting to talk with you." Travis said it slowly, like he was thinking it through, word by word.

"So you'll do this for me? You'll take me to the premiere tonight?" I was amazed; normally, a request like this would have cued in days of quarreling.

"It's red carpet, you know," he added. "You gotta dress."

"Heidi won't mind?"

"Heidi's working on a jigsaw puzzle of the Grand Canyon with Divinity. No jokes about that, please. She'll be fine."

112

"So we can do this? You'll take me to the premiere?"

"I'll have the limo there by six. Don't be late."

"I won't be, promise."

"Good," he said. "And when I see you maybe you can tell me why the hell you're so anxious to see a cartoon about a goddamn goldfish."

"You're the world's best ex-husband," I said as I shut off the phone and pulled into the parking structure for Santorini Spa. I wanted to see *Fool's Goldfish* because it was the easiest way I knew of to get to Palmer Collins. It was a premiere, he was one of the stars, and the evening promised to be very social. What easier way to talk to him than when his guard was down? Somehow, he fit into this puzzle about the murders; I was sure of it. Maybe it was his divorce from Rita; maybe it was his partnership with Luna. But it was something, and I wanted to find out what it was.

The receptionist at the spa was wearing a white silk toga and had a nimbus of blond hair, Boticelli's Venus reimagined for Rodeo Drive. "You're here for a noon appointment?" she asked.

"Yes, with Mr. Nikros." I looked around the reception room. It was painted with a huge mural of the Greek gods, Zeus, Apollo, Aphrodite, Poseidon, and the rest, on Mt. Olympus. But they weren't talking philosophy or sipping wine; instead, they were all engaged in various forms of love making. Zeus and Apollo were sharing Aphrodite's favors; Poseidon was going down on Hera. Goats watched from a hillside as Pan ravaged a more than willing Diana. The total effect of the room could best be described as Kama Sutra of the Gods.

"That will be five hundred dollars," said the receptionist with a warm smile that said "I'm here to take your money, that's all." She was wearing a pair of gorgeous Christian Laboutin sandals to go with the toga. Her perfectly manicured toenails had been painted coral; a gold toe ring encircled her second toe.

"No problem." I reached inside my purse and handed her Mary Kate's American Express card. She looked at it, then back at me. "I'm on her account," I said. "I'm her nutritionist."

The receptionist swiped the car once, then again. "The system seems to be down," she pouted.

"Does that mean I have to wait?"

"No,' she smiled. "If you let me hold the card, I can try it later. That way we can get you started right now." I nodded and she led me down a silent corridor that was marked by votive candles burning in small indentures in the wall. We reached a door with a mural of Circe painted on it. She was lying back on a cloud, pleasuring herself with a lute.

The receptionist ushered me in and handed me a thick, white terrycloth body towel. "Why don't you go ahead and change? Stavos will be in shortly."

A lavender candle burned in one corner of the room, casting a dim light and filling the room with a sweet, lush scent. A tape of the ocean was playing, the sound of the surf gently echoing against the walls, overlaid with the music of single flute. Wrapped in the towel, I lay down on the massage table, feeling relaxed already.

A moment later the door opened and Stavos walked in. He was wearing a knee length white cloth robe held in place, barely, by a poorly knotted sash. His caramel colored chest pressed against the fabric, with half of his right nipple discreetly revealed, a nosy neighbor peeking out from behind the curtain of decency.

"How is Mary Kate?" he asked as he reached over to a table, picked up some lotion and rubbed it between his thick hands.

"She's fine," I said, my head to the right side so I could see him. "She sends her love."

"I'm crazy about that woman," he said as he pulled my towel down to right above my butt. "She's one of a kind."

"Actually, there's another one just like her at home."

He chuckled. And then I felt his big hands grasp my shoulder blades and begin to knead them, his fingertips pressing deep into my sore muscles. Soon his knuckles were pressing against the base of my neck. First my flesh felt stressed, then a small tingle began to build, spreading down my spine.

"This is your first time here?" he asked, rubbing more of the lotion into my shoulders.

"Yes. But I've heard so much about your massage."

He chuckled again as his hands glided down to the bottom of my ribcage and began methodically working their way back up. "Yes. Everybody in Beverly Hills likes to be rubbed the right way."

I heard his cell phone vibrate in the pocket of his robe, but he ignored it. Then the music changed. The sound of the surf was replaced by soft rock, first *Baby I'm-A-Want You* by Bread, then *What a Fool Believes* by the Doobie Brothers. The music and Stavos' magic fingers strumming on my spine really brought it all back for me. Before I met Travis I had hung out with the Doobie Brothers and even slept with one of them. Not Michael

McDonald, he was taken, but one of the bearded guys. Actually, I reflected, they all pretty much had beards, so that wasn't helping me. The sweet rhythms of the song lulled me. "What a fool believes he sees/Is always better than nothing." I racked my brain for the answer. Stavos kept massaging me deeper and deeper, and the song kept building, but I just couldn't recall which Doobie I'd done.

Then the music changed again. This time it was Ravel's *Bolero* pouring softly, but insistently, through the speakers. Stavos undid his robe and hung it on the back of a chair. All he was wearing now was a tight white Speedo. I heard his cell phone vibrate again in the robe pocket, but it wasn't the only thing in the room that was moving. From the look of his Speedo, Stavos had sprinkled some Viagra on his Wheaties this morning.

He got up on the table, hovering over me in a squat position, his hands above my shoulders, his knees touching my thighs. "Relax," he whispered softly. Then he lowered himself on to me, his perfectly muscled flesh pressing down on my body. *Bolero* built higher and higher on the sound system as Stavos moved against me, his hard body, and I mean to tell you it was hard all over, churning against mine. So this was the five hundred dollar massage that all the ladies in Beverly Hills were paying for: now I understood. We had done this for free when we were in high school. Back then we used to call it dry humping.

Suddenly there was a knock on the door. Stavos continued grinding against me, but the knocking continued.

He raised himself off my body. "Please excuse me," he said softly. "I'll be right back."

He opened the door and spoke with someone in the hallway. Whoever it was said, "She wants you to call her back right away. She says there's an emergency with the tapes. She said you'd know what she meant." I knew who was speaking. The coral nail polish and the gold toe ring gave it away.

Stavos closed the door behind him and came back over to me. He reached for my shoulders and massaged them deeply. "Something unexpected has come up,' he said softly, "so I want to give you a choice. You can either finish this massage with one of our other masseurs, or we can end it now and this is on the house."

"Really? That's very generous of you."

He shook his head and smiled. "I hate doing this to a new customer," he continued. "But I have an emergency I need to deal with. If you want to come back I'll finish you off for a reduced rate, three hundred."

"How nice," I replied.

"Now, if you'll excuse me," he said, pulling his robe back on and digging his cell phone out of the pocket. He tapped it, pressed it to his ear, and, as he left the room, said "Hi Lace."

I dressed quickly and departed, leaving Mary Kate's card with the receptionist, who was sure to return it to her. I didn't need Stavos to finish me off for three hundred bucks. I felt I was getting pretty close to the climax of all this without anybody else's help.

16

Before I start a book, I make an outline. The outline doesn't spell out everything – that would take away half the fun of writing, the things that happen along the way, the stuff you discover—but it does serve as a kind of road map for the book's action. I usually draw my outline as a tree, with my main character as the trunk and the other characters growing out of him or her like branches. This helps me keep track of my character's origins and their relationships to each other.

So when I got home from the spa I sat down with a piece of paper and began to outline what I knew about the two murders that had occurred in the past week. I drew Tamara as the tree trunk, with Joel as a major branch growing from her, and, in turn, Chloe as a smaller branch growing from Joel. Of course, then I had to sketch in Beverly as a branch connected to both Joel and Chloe. Stumped (sorry) for what do about Wendy, I decided to make her her own tree trunk, with Lev as a big, angry branch growing out of her middle. And since she and Tamara had been friends, I had their branches touch at the top. That still left me with Palmer and Rita Collins; since he was a major client of the Zeitgeist Agency, I had him branch off from Lev. And then I had to draw two branches from Palmer for both of his wives, Rita and Daria. That still left me with Laci, related to nobody but so close with Chloe that I drew her as a leaf on Chloe's branch, and then I had to put Stavos as a leaf attached to Laci's leaf. But I had forgotten Warren Leuup, who had been the divorce lawyer for both Lev and Palmer, so I sketched him in as some netting that joined their branches.

That took care of all the people, but there were still things I couldn't get into the picture. Vance Packer for one; Luna for another. And, small as they might be, what the hell was up with Chloe's earrings? Why had Tamara and Wendy each been wearing one when they were murdered?

I had no clue. When I looked at what I had drawn, it wasn't the kind of well-drawn tree that would lead me to the right branch, the correct answer, the killer. It was more like a big, messy overgrown Chia Pet that you would buy at Target. But only if you were desperate to fill up that space on your bookshelf where Linda Goodman's *Sun Signs* had once sat.

Why couldn't I fit all this together? Clearly, something was up with Laci and Stavos and Luna. Probably Vance Packer was involved, maybe Palmer and Daria were as well. But what had the receptionist been referring to when she talked to Stavos about "the tapes?" Did that have to do with Luna? And if it did, how did it relate to the murders of Tamara and Wendy? And what about...

I kicked my clothes off in frustration and slipped into the shower. Time to get ready for *The Fool's Goldfish* premiere. I let the warm water drum on my back, relaxing me almost as much as Stavos had with his magic fingers, and began to plan my outfit for tonight.

Dressing for the red carpet has become an extreme sport out here. What was once a fun dress up thing has been converted, thanks to the tabloids and the TV interviewers, into a lynching party conducted in Dolce and Gabanna. Joan Rivers was Mother Teresa compared to some of the commentators, most of them unemployed designers and fashion editors, who pick through the evening's clothes like buzzards let loose in the county morgue. In defense, all the young stars are now dressed by stylists, an elite corp of dress Nazis who push them into overpriced couture, stuff their feet into glitzy stiletto heels that practically constitute Chinese foot binding, and then primp their hair until it resembles a soufflé on steroids. Then they drape them in borrowed jewels and send them down the red carpet so some fool can stick a microphone in their face and ask, "Who are you wearing tonight?"

You know something? Audrey Hepburn never used a stylist in her life. Has there ever been anyone who could match her style?

But I had to dress for the premiere because I was going with Travis and he was certain to be on camera. I've never bothered with a stylist, and I'm not one of those ladies who has a hundred outfits hanging in the closet. I prefer to buy a few great things and wear them sparingly. And I knew what I was going to wear this evening, a brown velvet Valentino gown with a plunging neckline accented by a gorgeous cream ribbon of silk. I'd bought it over ten years ago, but it looked as good now as it did back in the millennium days. I always say, stick with the classics, for me, that's Valentino and Armani, and you'll never go wrong. And I had just the pair of Jimmy Choo brown leather pumps, small bow on each side, to go with the gown.

"That looks familiar," said Travis as I settled next to him in the back seat of the limousine two hours later.

"So do you," I laughed, patting his cheek. "Thanks for taking me tonight."

"This is like old times. Remember when we went to the premiere of that Amazon movie you made?"

"*Amazon Honeymoon?*"

"That was it."

"There was no premiere for that one," I snorted. "More like a wake." *Amazon Honeymoon*, yet another of my 80s cinematic embarrassments, was a poor woman's *Romancing the Stone*, with me as a bride stranded in the rain forest and Lorenzo Lamas as the rogue helicopter pilot, they're always "rogue" in these movies, who saves me from a tribe of head hunters. Gene Simmons of Kiss made a very ill-advised film debut as my errant husband who wound up with his head on a stake at the end of the film. It was the only scene that drew any applause.

"Yes sir." Travis slipped his arm around me. "It's just like old times."

Travis and I have worked hard to remain friends in the years since our divorce, but this, the arm around the shoulder, was something new. He'd embraced me before, at Max's high school graduation, that day he came over and ate the brownies and I cried, but those had been different embraces, familial, if you will. This strong, broad arm encircling my bare shoulder, wasn't saying "You're family." More like, "You're still my woman."

Instinctively, I hunched my shoulder in a bit. "I think I'd be more comfortable... if we just sat next to each other."

Travis pulled his arm away and looked at me. "That what you did with the cop the other day?"

"So that's what this is about?" Damn Max and his big mouth!

"I just figured if you're handing out favors, I might get in line to get some with the rest of the crowd."

"If I want to kiss a man in my own house, it's my own damn business!" I blazed. Where did Travis get off talking to me like this?

"Guess so," he replied. "But I hate to think you might be giving our son ideas."

"Like our son has never had sex?" Men can be so incredibly thick at times.

"No, but I don't think he's ever seen his mother having sex. At least not yet."

"Oh, go to hell!" I shouted, scooting over to the far side of the limo.

"I just don't want you to be carrying on like one of those Hollywood moms," Travis said. "Like all that trash you see on the reality shows."

"And you're father of the year, huh? Married to Miss Tits for Brains who's so young you practically have to burp her before you screw her?"

"Watch your mouth. You're my wife."

"I *was* your wife. There's a difference."

He reached over and took my hand. "Nikki, in my mind, in some sort of weird way, we're always gonna be married. No matter who each of us winds up with. And so, as someone who still thinks of himself as your husband, I'm just asking you not to play around in public."

"You're jealous!" I said incredulously.

"Just don't embarrass me in public. That's all I ask."

I pulled my hand back from him. "Don't embarrass you in public? When we were married you used to close your show by singing a ballad to a dead goat that the band carried out on stage."

"That's different," Travis insisted. "That was entertainment."

"And you played around when we were married."

"That's a damn lie!"

"It is not. You played around and you know it."

"You never caught me."

"What about that wardrobe lady at the Head Bangers Ball in Serbia?"

Travis winced. "You know oral doesn't count. Besides, that was overseas."

I crossed my arms and glared at him. "Well this is on dry land, Travis. And if I want to do it again, I will. I'll kiss any cop I want, and you and your insane jealousy can't stop me."

Travis shook his head. "I'm not jealous. I'm protective. Of you."

"I don't need your protection anymore, thank you very much. I've done quite well for myself since the divorce. I've sold over ten million copies of my books. I run my own house, and I've raised Max. So back off."

Travis jerked his thumb towards Hollywood Boulevard, a mobius strip of pizza parlors, T shirt shops, and cigarette stores, separated from us by only a half inch of tinted limousine window glass. "It's a jungle out there, babe."

"Thanks, Tarzan," I snapped. "But I'll go it alone. And why don't you learn to deal with your jealousy? I mean, I've heard of jealous husbands, but jealous ex-husbands?"

He glowered at me. "You're calling me jealous after that stuff you said on the news last night?"

"Max told you that too?" I was appalled. When you can't trust your child to keep cheap gossip a secret, who can you trust?

"Running around in that phony wig. You looked like Stevie Nicks caught in the shower." Travis started to laugh.

"Well you ought to know," I shot back. "You showered with her enough."

"She's a clean living gal. You won't catch her on the Strip in a bad wig, spreading lies on the news."

"All of a sudden you've become Walter Cronkite?" I was steaming now. Travis actually had something on me.

"Hey, say whatever you want. But don't tell me you're not jealous when you start talking about Tori Spelling."

"That's nonsense," I snapped. "I was just having some fun with her."

"You were jealous as a wet hen, and you know it," Travis said smiling. "You have been for over two decades now."

"Ridiculous!"

"Balls," he chuckled. "You're jealous she beat you out for the part of Donna on *Beverly Hills 90210* and you have been for the past twenty years."

The truth! I was stung to the quick.

"She didn't deserve that role and you know it!" I blazed. "Everyone said I had it in the bag. The director, the head of casting, everyone. If godamned Tori hadn't told her ever-loving Daddy she wanted the role the night before shooting, I would have been in the biggest soap opera of the 90s."

There it was, out in the open. The reason I've always hated Tori Spelling. She took my damn part on what turned out to be one of the biggest television shows of all time.

"Nikki, they'd have never believed you as a virgin," said Travis. "That's why you lost the part."

"I lost the part because Tori Spelling was Aaron's daughter. No other reason. That woman has raised nepotism to an art form. She's the George W. Bush of entertainment!"

Travis smiled at me. "Are we finished now?"

But I wasn't. I couldn't help myself. "Travis, you don't understand because you did so well in music. I could have become a big star if I'd gotten that role."

"Oh yeah," he chuckled. "A big star. Just like Ian Ziering. What's he up to nowadays?"

I had to laugh. "Probably getting ready to do a hair replacement infomercial." Travis joined me in my laughter. "But I almost got that role, Travis. You know how much that hurts."

He reached over and took my hand again. "I know, babe. Guess we all have our private little jealousies, huh?"

I guess we do. Our limousine came to a stop and I looked out the window to see Graumann's Chinese and the crowd gathered around it. Several hundred people were lining both sides of the street, holding up cameras and cell phones, taking pictures as a stream of celebrities arrived. The exterior of Graumann's had been decorated with hundreds of tiny paper lanterns in the shape of goldfish, in honor, naturally, of "Fool's Goldfish." The lanterns, lit from within by tiny bulbs, were strung across the courtyard that had all the hand and footprints of the movie stars. The entrance into the auditorium was pretty much a concrete history of Hollywood; everyone from Clark Gable to Bruce Willis had been immortalized here. (Not me, of course. I mean, I might have been had I gotten that role on *Beverly Hills 90210* and then gone on to do a few… okay, I'll shut up about that. Promise.)

Graumann's Chinese is pretty much a tourist trap nowadays, but the façade, adorned with big red dragon heads and colored tile, is still tacky fun. Inside, it's another story. The theatre is so dimly lit, from a bunch of pagoda light fixtures, it's like stumbling into the ladies lounge at a bad Chinese restaurant. But that was ahead of us: right now Travis and I were on line for the red carpet.

A publicist from Zenith Studios, a young man who looked like Clay Aiken but with a decent haircut, came over, handed us some programs, and led us over to the VH1 interview station.

"They just want to speak with Travis, if that's okay with you," he said to me.

"Fine by me." I nodded as Travis sidled up to the interviewer. Behind them was a backdrop that consisted of the logos of the Kennedy Special Olympics and Luna, the two beneficiaries of the premiere, each of whom were getting fifty thousand dollars from Zenith for the evening.

"I've read every single one of your books, Miss Tyler," the publicist whispered to me.

"Thanks," I replied, giving him a hug. "I love to hear that."

"I've read them all too," said a voice behind me.

I turned around to see Vance Packer smiling at me, his porcelain veneers sparkling in the evening twilight.

"Do you know who I am?" I asked. "We've never really met."

He came up and put his arm around my waist as if we were long lost sweethearts at a high school reunion. "Of course I know who you are,

Nikki Tyler. You're the best selling Hollywood novelist in the world. Everybody reads your books."

"Even you?" I asked with a smile.

He swiped his hand over his chest, then raised it in the Boy Scout salute. "Every one, cross my heart."

I'd bet Vance hadn't cracked a book since *The Little Engine That Could* back in second grade, but I was impressed by his salesmanship. When you got right down to it, that's what he was all about. His group, Playerz, and the rest of the boy bands of the 90s hadn't really been about music. It was more about fancy dance moves, tight pants and a lots of hair gel. And the smiles, just like the one he was giving me now, the smiles really sold those boy bands. Now Vance was selling a different kind of music, Luna, music for mushheads, and the audience was bigger than it had been for him a decade ago.

"This is such a big evening for you," I said.

He looked around at the crowd, celebrities, agents, studio heads, all of them moving past the red carpet and into Graumann's. "It's a dream come true, Nikki. Everything we've been working on for over five years now."

A roar went up from the crowd as Palmer and Daria got out of their limo. Palmer turned to the other side of Hollywood Boulevard and waved to the crowd, which surged, lemming-like, against the wooden police barricades that security had erected earlier this afternoon.

"I understand Palmer has been very helpful to you," I said.

Vance nodded. "He's the best. A very spiritual guy. Very spiritual."

"How did he come to Luna?" I asked, trying to sound casual. "Was he having some sort of mid-life crisis?"

Vance gave me that new car salesman smile. "Hey, life is a crisis. That's what Luna is here for."

"Laci Stivers has been a big supporter too," I said.

"She'll be here tonight. She wouldn't miss this."

"With her boyfriend?"

"Oh yeah, Stavos will be with her. He's become a big supporter of ours as well."

I nodded. "Another very spiritual guy like Palmer?"

"Luna holds the key for many people, Nikki. Stavos is just one of them."

"It seems like you've really managed to reach men, like Palmer and Stavos," I pressed. "What's your secret?"

Vance favored me with a Zen-inspired gaze. "Luna acknowledges only one gender, Nikki. And that would be all humanity."

Another roar went up from the crowd as Laci, followed by Stavos, emerged from their limousine. She waved to the crowd, triggering a fusillade of flashbulbs and cell phone photos. Stavos stood discreetly beside her (I assumed the Viagra had worn off by now) as she began to shout out to crowd.

"I Love Laci!" she exclaimed, plugging her own dismal reality show. The crowd, in souvenir T-shirts, flip flops and muu-muus, cheered her on.

Then she pointed to the red carpet backdrop. "And I love Luna!" More cheering from the crowd.

"She's quite a good will ambassador for you," I said to Vance.

He surveyed the roaring crowd with satisfaction. "The people," he said softly. "They need a leader."

I shuddered as I thought about kind of people who might choose Laci Stivers as their leader. Whoever they were, tabloid-obsessed fans, shut-ins, paranoids convinced they had had relations with aliens, Vance seemed to want to tap into them. And why not? Nobody gives up their money quicker than the gullibles.

"You're doing so well right now," I said. "Better than you ever did with the music."

"That was an overture, you know?" he replied. "It was God's way of getting me ready to do this work, his work, right now."

"So you think Luna is God's work?"

"Absolutely. It's a gospel that is spreading faster every day."

"I heard you're moving into other cities," I said, thinking back to the speech he had made last night at No Exit.

Vance's face lit up at the prospect of his empire. "Totally. We are totally doing that. I said this to *People Magazine* when they interviewed me last week. Using Luna, I want to do for God what Starbucks did for coffee."

"You mean you want to overcharge for him?" I said.

He paused, then laughed, and gave me a big hug. "You know, I really like you, Nikki. You ought to come to one of our meetings at the Collins Center, see what we're all about."

And with that he was off to hug Laci and Stavos, who were still surrounded by paparazzi. I felt a hand slip into mine, Travis.

"Everything good with VH1?" I asked.

"Long as they don't use the footage in one of their wash-up shows," he grunted.

"Oh come on," I replied. "They've got you writing and singing a song for a huge animated movie. You're not washed up."

"You can be busy but washed up," replied Travis. "Ask Barry Manilow."

We were headed down the red carpet and into the theatre when a blond head bobbed in front of me. My nightly news nemesis, yet again.

"Travis Tyler and Nikki," cooed Lisa, sticking a microphone in front of us. "I thought you two were divorced."

"We stayed friends," said Travis.

"Like Bruce and Demi," I added, with a big, fat, insincere TV news smile.

"Or like Joel Osmond and his late wife Tamara," said Lisa with an even bigger smile, a Tony the Tiger on the Frosted Flakes box smile. "Nikki, I know you've been devastated by Tamara's murder. Have the police called you in for questioning?"

"We're just here for the movie," said Travis smoothly. "I wrote the title song."

"He sings it too," I added, through teeth that were gritted so hard I could practically feel them grinding.

"Well," rebounded Lisa, "so much has been happening for you two. The song in this wonderful movie. The murder of a close friend. And by the way who are you wearing?"

I wanted to say "You, I slaughtered and skinned you last night and now I'm wearing your flesh." I resisted.

"Valentino."

"It's gorgeous," said Lisa. "Did you work with a stylist on your look?"

"Actually, I worked with a friend of mine. Debbie Cakes."

Lisa's eyes widened perceptibly. I saw Travis suppressing a smile. "You're a friend of Debbie Cakes?" she asked suspiciously.

"For many years now," I replied.

Lisa's eyes narrowed. "When was the last time you saw her?"

"Just this afternoon."

"Where was she?" She was hanging on my every word.

"At the supermarket. Whole Foods."

"Whole Foods in Beverly Hills?" Lisa's big, round eyes, the eyes of a born newscaster, grew larger by the second.

"Yes. She was in the bakery aisle."

"The bakery aisle?"

I nodded. "She's probably still there."

"Thank you so much, Nikki." Lisa smiled as if, Sherlock Holmes-style she had cracked the case wide open. I pictured her running into Whole Foods with her camera crew at her side.

Travis tugged on my hand. "Come on babe, we don't want to be late for the movie."

17

Fool's Goldfish tuned out to be a sweet little children's fable about Stan, a special needs goldfish, voiced by Will Smith, who can't keep up with the rest of the students in First Fish Grade. One day he finds a treasure map hidden in a conch shell and decides to search for the hidden pirate's gold instead of attending school. He hooks up with Myrna, a tasty little scallop, voiced by Jessica Alba (natch), and they wind up being pursued by Rush Limbaw, a very fat, mean shark, voiced by Palmer. At the end of the film Rush Limbaw gets harpooned and the audience burst into applause as he died. I couldn't help wondering how that felt for Palmer.

Afterwards there was a big party at the Roosevelt Hotel, across the street from Graumann's. Back in the day, Marilyn Monroe had lived at the Roosevelt for two years and it was considered to be a glittering icon, a home for the bad and the beautiful. Then Hollywood Boulevard fell on hard times and the Roosevelt slid from movie goddess status to a rouged-up hooker, turning tricks for the tourists to keep the doors open. It was revamped a few years ago, and though a lot of it still reeks of 70s tack, they've come up with the poolside Tropicana Bar that attracts a lot of young Hollywood. Palm trees surround a big blue pool where, if you believe the legend, Marilyn once posed for a magazine spread on the diving board. That's where the party was.

"Movie parties are always swankier than music parties," mused Travis.

He got that right. This party was being sponsored by Commander's Reserve, a new British gin that was trying to break into the American market. Everywhere you looked bartenders were shaking up batches of gin and Rose's Lime Juice, pouring them into cocktail glasses and handing them to the waiters to distribute to the crowd. Meanwhile somebody had thought to put little fishbowls, the kind you used to win at carnivals when you were a kid, on every table. And in each one was a darling little goldfish.

The photo op area was over by the pool. That's where I saw Vance and Palmer posing together for a picture. What happened next stunned me a bit: Lev Strasser joined them, threw his arms around them, and the three of them posed for a series of shots.

Travis gave a low whistle. "His wife's not even close to cold yet."

"Palmer's his biggest client," I replied. "You know Lev. Nothing gets in the way of business."

But there was a bigger surprise in store. A moment later Warren Leuup, the divorce lawyer of your nightmares, joined the group for still another round of photos. *Murderer's Row*, I thought to myself.

"Kind of like the four horsemen, huh?" I turned to see Joel standing behind us.

"What are you doing here?" I asked. "Don't tell me you're involved with this Luna business too."

He shook his head. "I'm here for Palmer. He asked me to come. Besides, it's good to get out of the house. I've been…" He trailed off but you could see the hurt Joel seemed to be carrying for Tamara.

I hooked my arm through his. "Join us." As I did the Zenith publicist with the Clay Aiken hair bobbed up again.

"Mr. Tyler, can I grab you for an interview with *E Entertainment?*"

"I guess," grumbled Travis as he was led away.

"Remember who you're wearing," I shouted over my shoulder. A waiter was passing by and I grabbed two drinks for Joel and myself. We settled in at a small table, the captive goldfish swimming between us.

"How are you doing?" I asked.

He shrugged. "You know, a day at a time." Joel picked up his cocktail and took a sip. I joined him.

"Gin and lime juice," I said as my mouth puckered up. "The best medicine."

He looked around at the crowd, the pool, and all the party trimmings. "Success is the best medicine. Everything else comes second."

I gestured towards the Four Horsemen. "Can you believe Lev showed up?"

"It's a big night. And he's represented Palmer for almost twenty years now. How could he stay home?"

"You think he's in mourning?"

Joel glanced at him. "No, I think he's in Armani. Besides, however shocked he may have been over Wendy's death, I don't know that he's exactly sorry about it."

"Because?" This was one answer I had to hear.

He paused and took another sip of his drink, deciding whether or not to spill the beans. "I heard it was all over between them. They were getting a divorce."

"You think that's why Warren Leuup is here tonight?"

"Who knows why the hell he's here. Maybe he's looking for new clients. You don't have to look that hard for people who want to get divorced in this town."

The gin and lime juice were beginning to have that warm and wavy effect on my thinking. Which is probably why I dared to ask Joel a question I'd been wondering about for several days.

"Did you know Warren Leuup's name was written in Tamara's manuscript, the one you gave me?"

He nodded. "Yeah, I saw it there. Don't ask me why."

"It doesn't make any sense really. She had no reason to contact him. You two were already divorced."

He finished his drink. "We never should have gotten divorced. That was our problem."

"How's Chloe?"

"You heard about the dust-up she got into last night? At No Exit?"

"That's why I asked."

"She got into an argument with the bouncer and he pulled a gun on her. You believe that?"

"Did she tell you what the argument was about?"

He shrugged. "He was giving her attitude so she gave it back to him. Then the bum pulls a gun on her." Joel motioned with his thumb over to the photo area. "They all act like big deals since *The Sopranos. The Godfather* was over by the eighties but now they've all come back."

I saw who Joel was talking about. A stout little man with a puffed out chest, dressed in a black turtleneck and an ice blue suit jacket. And tinted sunglasses, of course. It was Sal Bucatti, "bodyguard" to the stars. I put the word bodyguard in quotes because the term was just a formality, like the women who called Stavos Nikros a masseur when he was really just a whore. Sal Bucatti was a fixer. If you were rich and famous and had a problem, the kind of problem you didn't want to talk to the police about, Sal Bucatti was the man you called. He started out as security for Frank Sinatra and wound up as an advisor to Michael Jackson. Rumor had it he and his associates could tap anyone's phone through a high tech computer system and a series of connections to everyone from the phone company to the LAPD. What wasn't a rumor was that Sal had been indicted numerous times for everything from assault to wire fraud to extortion, and he'd beaten the rap every time.

Sal's m.o. was to come up to you, slip a piece of hard candy in your palm and say "How's it going?" The candy was supposed to let you know that he meant no harm. He kept an entire side pocket filled with cellophane wrapped butterscotch and strawberry candies. And now he was here, at a big premiere event for Luna. Had Sal gotten religion?

"I liked it better when they used the Russian mob," Joel said with a crooked grin.

"But Chloe's okay?" I asked, wishing that he would tell me what last night's shooting at No Exit had been all about.

"Yeah, she's fine. She's been a great help to me. No matter what problems she had with Tamara, she's always been my girl. In fact, I always thought that was what the big deal was about. She resented Tamara, resented that, as my wife, she had a closeness with me that Chloe could never share."

"Daddy's girl," I said as I polished off my drink.

Joel grinned. "Oh yeah, always has been. Even the men she dates."

"Chloe's got a boyfriend?" I was surprised. Every time we'd talked it seemed to me Chloe was bemoaning the lack of a beau.

"Not a boy. A man. She's always liked them older."

"Have you met him?'

Joel shook his head. "She won't introduce me. Not yet. Just told me that there's someone in her life and he's not as old as I am."

"That leaves the field open," I said.

"Damn right." Joel threw back his head and laughed.

It was nice to see my old friend coming back to life. "Another drink?"

"Nah, I've done my bit for Palmer. I'm going to disappear." He leaned over and kissed me on the cheek. "How about you?"

Looking across the pool I saw that Palmer was finally finished having his picture taken. I reached out and grabbed a drink off the nearest waiter's tray. "I'm going to run the gimlet," I said returning Joel's kiss.

"Have fun."

The thing you need to remember about approaching an actor is that there's one thing they all respond to: total adoration. Anyone who chooses to make their living having their face plastered across a giant screen in a dark room is a pretty good bet to be a sucker for flattery.

Palmer was surrounded by a small throng of publicists, for both Zenith Pictures and Luna. I shimmied right through the crowd and handed him the drink I'd just scored.

"You look fantastic!" I raved.

He beamed and gave me a hug. "You too, my love."

"And the movie!" I gushed. "Your voice was so…"

"Audible?" he said, his eyes lighting up with that million dollar twinkle that movie stars seem to be born with. It was the perfect dry comment for a job that required standing in a sound booth for two weeks imitating a shark and then collecting a two million dollar paycheck for it. Me, I'd have voiced a sardine for a mere ten thousand, but, alas, my name has no marquee value and Zenith Pictures hadn't come a calling.

"I had no idea you were so involved with Luna," I said. "When did it all begin?"

"I turned to Luna when I was making *Thunder Over Bethlehem*." He bowed his head as he said it, whether it was for Luna or the mere mention of the movie he had directed, I couldn't tell.

"But that was such a deeply Christian film," I said.

"I was deeply Christian when I made it." He turned on the million dollar twinkle again. When in doubt, flirt; that's the movie star motto. And it usually works.

"So when did that change?"

"Nikki, *Thunder Over Bethlehem* was more than a movie for me. It was a life changer. I had come to Christianity, but I knew my marriage was falling apart. I cast Daria as Mary and it turned into my own personal Virgin Birth."

Unable to respond to this—only a Hollywood star could equate his adultery with the birth of Christ – I reached for the only logical next question. "Where is Daria?"

"She's over there with the kids." Palmer proudly pointed to the opposite side of the pool. Daria was posing for pictures with a group of very well-dressed young children.

"They're the children of Luna members," he continued. "Most of us have come to this as a second, or even third, religion. But these children have been born into it. Daria is a volunteer at their pre-school."

"So Luna helped you divorce Rita and move on to Daria?" It was a rude question, but I had to ask it.

"Oh no. Luna taught me something much more essential. You see, when I was directing *Thunder Over Bethlehem*, I had begun to feel I was all powerful. I had put up all the financing, I was directing the film, then I fell in love with my leading lady. My ego was completely out of control, which probably did hurt my marriage to Rita. It was Luna, which Daria is a founding member of, that brought me back to reality. Luna taught me humility. And I needed that bring down. It was like I was making a film about the birth of Christ and I had developed my own Messiah complex."

131

"How strange," I murmured, "an actor who thinks he's God."

He sniffed the air around us. "Do I detect the scent of cheap irony?"

"It's my favorite perfume. I wear it to all my premieres."

That earned me a hug and the twinkle. Flirt, flirt, flirt. Palmer still knew how to lay it on.

"It's been such a journey for you," I said. "From born again Christian to Luna. I mean it's really fascinating."

"I understand your new book is about an actor who undergoes a religious conversion." Somewhere in the distance I heard a reel being cast and a fly hitting the water. Fishing had begun.

"Well yes, but as you know it's totally fictional, like all my books."

"Like the one about the female pop star who can't really sing that well but sleeps with everyone to get to the top and then starts adopting African children?" Palmer arched his left eyebrow, doing his best Cary Grant.

"You mean *Venus in Leather*?" I replied. "I'll have you know that I got a note from Madonna saying she loved that book. The new one, *Malibu Bad Boy* is about a drunken superstar who's an anti-Semite and a Holocaust denier. He sees the light when he falls in love with an Israeli secret agent.'

"Well then that couldn't be me, could it?" he said smoothly. "You know I've never been anti-Semitic."

"I know that, Palmer. This book isn't about you any more than it's about Mel Gibson."

He broke out into smile. "Hey, at the very least, being anti-Semitic is very bad business."

"Agreed," I said. "Ever wonder why almost everyone in show business is Jewish?"

"Probably because Hitler hated the theatre," he replied, and I had to laugh again.

"What's so funny?" It was Doria, who had finished her photo session and was now officially back at Palmer's side.

"Nothing much," I said. "We were just talking about old times.'

"That must have been fun," she replied. The sincerity of Doria's delivery offered ample proof why she had not been offered a single film role since finishing her stint as Mary in *Thunder Over Bethlehem*. She looked over at the glass I had handed Palmer, which was now empty. "I haven't even had a drink."

"Let's take care of that," he said. "Catch you later, Nikki."

"Thanks, Palmer." I looked around for Tyler or a waiter with another drink, either would do. Then suddenly I felt something slip into my hand.

"How's it going?" I had a hard candy in my palm and Sal Bucatti in my face.

I put the candy down on the table in front of us. "I'm on a diet."

"Sugar's good for someone as sweet as you," he oozed.

"Well if I'm so sweet, why do I need the sugar?"

Never the swiftest, Sal had to think about this for a second. "Oh, I get it. Well, then, how about this?" He unwrapped the candy and dropped it in the fishbowl that was on the table. "Maybe the goldfish will like it."

"Sal, that candy is going to dissolve in there. The sugar could kill the fish."

"We wouldn't want that, would we?" I couldn't tell if he was threatening me or just being droll, a word I'm sure he'd never come across in his life. But Sal surprised me. He pushed up his jacket sleeve, reached into the fishbowl, and pulled out the candy.

"My good deed for the day." He smiled.

"You always do good deeds?"

"I'm here aren't I?"

"I didn't know you were a follower of Luna, Sal." Now I was the one who was fishing.

"Let's say. I support the people who follow it. Good people like Vance Packer and Palmer. I support them and I'd hate to have anything bad said or written about them."

A waiter came by and put a fresh drink on the table. I picked it up and took a sip. "Why would you think I'd write anything bad about them?"

He took off his blue-tinted sunglasses and polished them. Without bothering to look up, he kept talking. "Oh, I don't know. You see somebody asking a lot of questions, you kind of begin to wonder why they're doing that."

I took another sip of the drink for courage. "I'm a writer. I always ask questions. It's my job." Where the hell was Tyler?

Sal slipped his sunglasses back on. "Sometimes people should take a vacation from their job. It's good for them."

Why was this two-bit thug trying to intimidate me? With each threat, my back went further up. "I rarely take vacations, Sal. I'm a very hard worker. Always have been."

He looked me dead in the eye. "Time to see a travel agent."

"Or?" I couldn't help myself.

Sal reached into the fishbowl and grabbed the goldfish. He dumped the poor flopping fish on the table. Then, in one clean motion, he reached into his suit jacket, pulled out a switchblade knife, flicked it open, and drove the blade of the knife right through the fish.

"They don't live that long anyway," he said with a smile.

I threw my drink in his face. "Longer than you should, you lousy bastard." It was a cheap, melodramatic gesture, right out of one of those bad Aaron Spelling shows I'd never been cast in. And it felt great.

18

"**You** gonna be all right, babe?"

Travis was worried about me, and I was touched. He'd seen me douse Sal Bucatti, and all the way home he'd been fretting. Now we were parked in my driveway, like teenagers on a first date. Which was kind of ironic when you consider that our first date back in the 80s had started out with a tequila soaked dinner at Dan Tana's and wound up in a penthouse suite at the Hyatt House.

"I'll be fine. You don't have to worry about me."

He put his hand over mine. "But I do. Force of habit."

"Sal Bucatti's just a schoolyard bully with a lifetime supply of Aqua Velva. He's not going to come after me, a defenseless woman."

"I sure hope not. You know, even with Heidi and Divinity and everything, you're part of the family."

I leaned over and gave Travis a big long hug. "You're sweet. I'll be fine."

I got out of the car and headed up the walk to my door as Travis yelled, "Call if you need me." All the while I rationalized my behavior at the premiere. Bucatti was a big fat beast, and cruelty to animals was a huge no-no in my book. He'd actually laughed at me when I threw the drink in his face, then picked up a napkin, wiped himself off, and walked away. Oh, and before he did, he handed me another hard candy.

I knew he was an enforcer, but that was for other people. And, for all the wiretapping he'd done for blue blood lawyers, lawyers who always denied knowing him. Sal Bucatti had never been arrested for any violent act that I knew of. True, a couple of years ago, when another rapper was mad at Kanye West, rumor had it Bucatti sent Kanye a forty pound catfish dressed in Victoria's Secret lingerie. It was supposed to be a reminder that you never know when you may be sleeping with the fishes. But Kanye, never the brightest bulb on the Christmas tree, was reported to have invited over one hundred of his nearest and dearest friends and thrown the fish fry to end all fish frys.

For all my rationalizing, I double-locked the front door on my way in and called our local protection service, Bel Air Patrol, to ask them to circle by the house several times during the night. That was enough to get me a decent night's sleep, and by morning I was at the computer. I should have been having a go at the last pages of *Malibu Bad Boy*, but I had something more important to look into.

I googled Luna and Vance Packer and the search brought me right to the organization's home page. There was an audio feed with testimony from Luna followers and a series of alternating graphics that featured photographs of the Collins Center as well as crowd shots from recent Luna meetings. But that just told me what I already knew; Luna was a coming thing, very popular. It was when I clicked on "Who We Are" that I hit the motherlode.

The Board of Directors tab brought me to a list of over twenty names. Four of them stood out immediately: Vance Packer, Palmer Collins, Lev Strasser and Warren Leuup. The quartet who had been posing for all the pictures last night; the group Joel had called The Four Horsemen. *What* did they have in common? Something stronger than Luna had to be holding together an ex-boy band singer, a movie star, an agent, and a big time divorce lawyer.

Stuck for an answer, I picked up the phone and called Beverly. She was the best in I had to Rita Collins, and Rita was someone I wanted to talk to, someone who might have some answers.

"Hey it's Nikki. How are you?"

I could tell by the slight pause that she was a little surprised to hear from me.

"Oh fine," said Beverly. "Except everyone I know keeps getting murdered. I'm practically afraid to leave the house."

"Well, so far they're only murdering second wives."

"Guess I'm safe then," chuckled Beverly, who had never remarried after she and Joel split up. "Actually, what I'd really like is a second husband. I think I ought to go out and get me a gubby."

"A gubby?" That was one I hadn't heard before.

"Yeah," she continued. "A gubby. A gay hubby. You know, meet some handsome little estate planner or designer who's tired of all the flashy West Hollywood boys and wants to settle down with a woman who can take care of him. We can go to the theatre together, and to benefits, and on weekend we can have all his ex-boyfriends over for cocktails."

"What about sex?" I asked.

"What about it? I last had it back in 1995 and I distinctly recall it being overrated. Beside, you get to cuddle with a gubby."

"You're too much."

"Listen, a lot of women out here are married to gubbies. Some of them even realize it." I could hear Beverly climbing out of bed, rummaging around at her vanity. At least my call had stirred her.

"I don't think you're the gubby type, Beverly. You'd probably turn the poor guy straight and then you'd wind up having to have sex with him."

"Nonsense," she replied. "Look at Liza Minnelli. She keeps marrying gubbies all the time, and I hear she's had less sex than a praying mantis."

"Don't they kill their mate when they have sex?"

"There you go. Now why have you called me, Nikki?" It wasn't confrontational; just Beverly's usual blunt style of conversation.

"I need a favor from you. A biggie."

Beverly chuckled. "What do I get in return?"

"What do you want?"

"Well I told you I wanted a gubby, but you don't seem up for that. What else have you got?"

"How about I dedicate my next book to you?"

"Hmm, I haven't had an offer like that since I went down on Dickens."

"Done!" I declared as I choked back my laughter. Beverly really did have the meanest, funniest mouth north of Wilshire.

"One thing, though. I don't want it to be some damn children's book. I want a real live, big, fat best seller."

"You have my word," I promised, thinking guiltily of *Malibu Bad Boy.*

"Now what's your favor?"

"I'd like to meet for lunch today at the Polo Lounge. And I'd like you to bring Rita Collins with you."

"I can do that. Rita has never had the nerve to refuse me anything."

"And then, at a certain point, I need you to disappear to the ladies room so Rita and I can have a private chat."

"Every word of which you'll tell me when I call you later."

"You drive a hard bargain."

"Make the reservation for one," said Beverly. "And use my name. We'll get a better table."

* * * *

Beverly may have been a bitch, but she was right. The hostess led me to a table on the terrace with a perfect view of both the lawn and George Clooney, who was lunching with his lawyer. Joel, on his way out, stopped by my table.

"Are you coming here for lunch every day now?" he asked.

"I'm not quite in your tax bracket yet. More like every other day."

"Who are you meeting?"

"Your ex-wife."

Joel stared off into the distance; nothing registered on his face. "Give her my regards," he said as he left.

Javier was at my side a moment later. "Something to drink while you wait?"

I wanted to order a martini, but I had a serious conversation coming up. "I'll just have an ice tea today, thanks."

"And, of course, the…"

"The McCarthy salad, dressing on the side."

Javier smiled, showing a pair of perfect dimples. "Always with you, no?"

"Yes, always. But wait until my guests arrive and order. For now, why don't you just bring a cheese plate?"

I was spreading a nice, runny glob of brie over a cracker when I looked up and saw Beverly and Rita approaching the table. Beverly must have managed to make it to the hairdresser, because her blond helmet was in place. But Rita looked frail, almost gaunt, especially when she walked into the afternoon sun. They sat down at the table and Javier returned.

"Something to drink?" he asked.

Rita pursed her lips, sighed and said, "I'd like a Bloody Mary. But very bloody, lots and lots of tomato juice."

"Certainly." Javier looked over to Beverly.

"I'll take a Bloody Mary too. But very merry. Lots and lots of vodka."

I ordered my martini and popped the cracker in my mouth. As I did, Rita let out a soft gasp. "You're eating the skin!"

"What?" I was mystified.

"Of the brie," she replied. "You're eating the skin of the cheese."

"I always do," I replied.

Rita's eyes began to glow with a small, soft fire, her first sign of real life. "My nutritionist told me all about this. The skin is the part of the milk that the cheese has refused. And if the cheese has refused it, why wouldn't you?"

"Oh, I've eaten skin before," I replied as I popped the cracker in my mouth.

Beverly suppressed a grin as Javier brought over the drinks and we toasted. "To three middle-aged dames," she said. Which was true of Beverly, if she planned to live to be 125 years old.

"So how is everything?" I asked. "How's Chloe? Is she okay after that incident in the nightclub?"

Beverly waved her hand dismissively as she swirled her straw in the Bloody Mary and took a long, long sip. "Couldn't be better," she said coming up for air. "The whole thing was a misunderstanding with some rent-a-thug. The police aren't pressing charges against her and our lawyer is handling the rest. It was a benefit for a religion, for God's sake."

"Everything seems to be about Luna right now," I said casually. Rita stiffened as I did, but not Beverly. She waved her hand for a second time.

"It's just something new for the kids, the newest fad, the hip religion," she said. "No different from us when we were younger. Joel and I practiced Zen Buddhism in the early seventies. Had a meditation mat, did the chanting, the whole bit."

"Buddhism is a real religion," said Rita, showing some of the same distaste she had shown for my cheese eating habits. "Luna…" She paused, seeming to measure her words. "Luna is just a crock."

Beverly waved her hand a third time, like a sorceress granting wishes. "Speaking of which, I think I'll have the onion soup for lunch."

I turned to Rita. "Have you been involved in Luna?"

She paused again. "Not involved. No."

"But you know about it?"

"Well Palmer's given them a couple millions dollars. He could have given that to me."

Rita, studying the menu, let out a low, soft whistle. "Maybe I'll have the crab cakes instead."

"I guess you must miss the money," I said.

"Sometimes I even miss Palmer," Rita replied softly.

Beverly reached over and patted her hand. "Reets, we've all had our bad moments with men and with alimony. The point is we're here, it's a lovely day, and the crab cakes are killer. Let's have fun."

Rita pulled her hand away. "I don't eat crab, or any kind of fish or animal flesh, in case you've forgotten. And besides, I lost so much in the settlement, I couldn't really afford the crab cakes here, unless they were an appetizer."

"Let me suggest the field greens, then. They're organic and quite reasonable." It was Javier, bless him, bringing a note of sanity to the proceedings.

We ordered our food and went back to our drinks. Beverly reached across the table for the cheese plate.

"Give me some of that skin," she growled.

"What I don't understand," I said, "is why Luna has such a hold on everybody. The pitch is it's supposed to help you make money. They sell distributorships like Amway. But Laci Stivers has all the money in the world. Her family's so real estate rich they could buy Donald Trump. What's Luna got that she wants?"

Beverly perked up. "That's an easy one. Ever see that ridiculous cable show of hers, *I Love Laci*?"

I nodded. "She and all those girls on E!, like the Kardashians, are giving stupidity a bad name. I can't believe they keep it on the air."

"They keep it on the air because Vance Packer is underwriting the entire cost of it with some of the loot he's made from Luna. So of course Laci loves him and his religion. He's her sponsor."

This was news to me. "But do they run commercials for Luna during the show?"

Beverly shook her head. "It's all hush-hush. The whole show's a vanity job for Laci, with Vance footing all the bills. The point of it that she gets to act like a star, her fantasy, everybody's fantasy. In return, she's a spokesperson for Luna. He bought her, just like Charmin bought Mr. Whipple."

"Who told you this?"

"Joel. He tells me everything." She said it with a certain smugness, as if to remind us that, even after a divorce, Beverly had an in with one of the biggest producers in town.

"Well I don't care how rich Laci Stivers is," said Rita as she picked at her greens. "I think she's a dumb little slut." What else would she have said considering that Laci had slapped her at Tamara's funeral?

"Yes," I replied, "she was beastly to you the other day, wasn't she?"

Rita's eyes began to fill with tears. "I heard that Laci started doing drugs at ten. She used to give grass to all her girlfriends at Crossroads. When they called up her parents, they just switched her to another school."

"That's terrible," I said. "Who told you that?"

"Someone who knows her very well," Rita replied carefully. She clearly wasn't going to give up the name that easily. "I also heard from the same person that Laci lost her virginity to her second cousin when she was fourteen. And he was eleven."

"There's no substitute for a bad childhood," chimed in Beverly before taking another swig of her Bloody Mary. Then she rose out of her chair and gave me a knowing look. "Will you both excuse me? I've got to visit the little girl's room."

"What's keeping you busy these days?" I asked Rita.

She shook her head slowly. "Nothing much. This vegan diet, for whatever it's worth."

Plain old sad was the word for Rita. With her skinny frame and her shag haircut she looked like a little sparrow that had lost its way back to the nest. Clearly the divorce from Palmer, and its aftermath, had been weighing on her. I sympathized, but I knew I had to go in for the kill.

"Maybe you should try a massage," I suggested.

She looked surprised. "Why would I do that?"

"I had one the other day, and it was the best massage I've had in my entire life."

Rita looked quite wary.

"Everyone kept telling me about this great guy at the Santorini Spa, and, boy, were they ever right. This guy does all the middle-aged broads in this town. Hasn't missed a one. And it was expensive, but, I've got to tell you, Rita, it was worth every penny. When he crawled on top of me and began rubbing his body on mine I just had to yell out, "Stavos, baby, you're making me…""

"Stop it!' Rita was red and shaking, the tears running down her face. "Stop it right now!"

"You know him?"

She buried her face in the napkin for a second, then threw it to the side. "Of course I know him. You mean you didn't know I knew Stavos? You and "every other middle aged broad in this town?""

"I'm sorry," I said quickly. "I thought he was just a hot masseur. I didn't know you and he were…"

"Involved?" said Rita. "Yes, we were, a couple of years ago. It started out as just a diversion, but then, what can I tell you Nikki, I really fell for him. We spent time together, lots of it. We shared our thought, our feelings, even secrets".

"So this was the real thing?"

Rita laughed with an undertone of bitterness I'd never thought she was capable of. "I certainly thought so. I was trying to figure out a way to leave Palmer for him."

"Well, you did leave Palmer, didn't you?"

She shook her head slowly, as if the knowledge of all this was too much to bear. "No, I didn't leave Palmer. He ended up leaving me. For

Daria Belson, no less. And then Stavos moved on. So I got left high and dry."

"Who did he move on to?"

"Wendy Strasser. Among others."

I clucked sympathetically. "Stavos really is a bad boy, isn't he? Leading you on like that. What a creep."

This seemed to bring her back to life. "No, you're wrong," she insisted. "He's done bad things, but he's not bad. Laci Stivers is the one who's bad."

"And he's the one who told you all about her, right?"

She nodded. "She's evil. He told me everything. Before they were involved. He knew all about her from the clubs."

"Is he still in love with you?"

This brought forth another small Niagara of tears. "No, no," wailed Rita into her napkin. "I wish he was. I tried to get him back. But he's moved on. First to Wendy, then to Laci. She bankrolled his spa. She bought his love, that little bitch."

I clucked sympathetically to the kind of line I would have been paid millions to say had I gotten that role on *90210*. "And you want it back?" She nodded. "Which is why Laci slapped you at the funeral?"

Rita looked down at her lap; she seemed utterly forlorn. "Well, I suppose you could say I was... stalking him. I kept calling. That's why she slapped me."

I reached over and held her hand the way Beverly had. "Oh, dear Rita. I think you're out of your league dealing with Laci Stivers. You're better off leaving Stavos to her."

Rita wiped her tears away and composed herself. "That's not all there is to it. She's involved with Luna, there's a whole thing going on. I can't talk about it."

Now we were getting somewhere. "But why not, Rita? What kind of control does Luna have over you? How can they hurt you?"

She jumped up and grabbed her purse. "Stay away from them, Nikki. Laci, Stavos, Luna, the whole bunch of them. They're poison." Rita turned sharply and sped across the terrace. She almost knocked over Beverly who was coming back from the ladies room. Beverly watched Rita speeding away, then surveyed the table and the crumpled napkin.

"Did I come in after the credits?" she asked.

19

On my way home, steering my beloved Bentley across Sunset, my cell phone rang.

I picked it up and heard a husky male voice. "How've you been?" It was Detective Stefano.

"How did you get this number?"

"I'm a policeman, remember? An investigator."

I had to smile. "I seem to recall that."

"So, long time no see."

"A couple of days."

"Except I saw you on television. When you were at No Exit, being interviewed by that TV bimbo. Debbie Cakes. That was pretty funny."

"How could you tell that was me?"

"I used to work in missing persons. That was a terrible wig you were wearing."

"That wig cost a fortune," I fumed. "It was supposed to make me look like Stevie Nicks."

"She's not that desperate." He laughed.

It was good to hear from the Detective again. Just the sound of his voice gave me a tiny frisson.

"So, is your son still around?"

"No, he's back at school."

"Want some company?"

He came over at six, dressed in an Aerosmith T-shirt and a pair of jeans. "That's not my husband's band," I said when I opened the door.

"I thought you told me you were divorced." The tiniest flicker of a grin was perking up the far corners of his mouth.

I led him into the house. "How about you, Detective..."

"Rocco," he corrected me.

"Rocco," I continued, glad for the reminder. "Have you ever been married?"

"No, but I try to make it a habit to be faithful to the woman I'm with. That count for anything?"

We were in the kitchen by now. "It makes you better than about half the married men I know. You didn't bring any food did you?"

He shoved his hands in his back pockets and brought them out empty. "Seem to have forgotten that."

"Well, I had a big lunch. How hungry are you?"

He shrugged. "We could order something."

Inspiration struck. "Wait," I said. I opened the door to the refrigerator and searched through the shelves. "Do you like Cool Whip?"

"Who doesn't?"

I pulled out the container and grabbed a couple of plastic spoons, the kind you use at picnics. "Here, we can have some Cool Whip."

"For dinner?" he said. "You're serving me Cool Whip as the main course?"

I handed him a spoon. "Shut up and eat." We sat on opposite sides of the counter, spooning the creamy stuff into our mouths. What is it about Cool Whip that tastes so good? Probably all the chemicals.

Rocco reached over and handed me a package. "I finished your friend's book."

"What did you think?"

"You were right, it's pretty poor. But I was interested in the heroine. She was a real bad girl. Do you think it could have been anyone Tamara Osmond knew?"

"There are two obvious candidates," I said, licking some Cool Whip off the back of the spoon. "Chloe Osmond, her stepdaughter, and Laci Stivers, Chloe's pal. They both have party girl reputations. And Chloe always resented Tamara. Tamara used to deny it, but it was true. There was no love lost there."

Rocco had switched into his investigator mode. "And Chloe resented Tamara because?"

I shrugged. "The obvious assumption is that Tamara replaced her in Joel's affections. Chloe was very much a daddy's girl; Joel doted on her. When Tamara came on the scene, that changed."

"And Laci Stivers?

"The bad news never stops with her." I dug in for one more spoonful. "She dropped out of school at sixteen and has been living at the clubs on the Sunset Strip ever since. You can chart her progress by looking at the tabloids every weekend at the supermarket. She's got lots of money, but she's also got lots of enemies."

"So why didn't somebody kill her?" he asked.

"They haven't had time yet?" I guessed.

"In the book, the girl winds up committing suicide."

"Yes, I thought that was wishful thinking of Tamara's part. She always was a bit of a cockeyed optimist."

144

Rocco grinned. "You quote *South Pacific?*"

I grinned right back. "You *know* *South Pacific?*"

"My last girlfriend was a professor of musical comedy at a community college. She taught me everything."

"We must do a revival of *The Music Man* someday," I replied.

"After we solve these murders," he said.

"Oh yes," I agreed. "We've got to do that first. What if the book isn't the cause of all this? Maybe Tamara just finished writing it, and then, for reasons that had nothing to do with it, someone killed her. After all, the same person killed Wendy Strasser, and she didn't write a book."

"So where's the motive?"

I sighed. "I have no idea. But there has to be a link between Tamara and Wendy, something we don't know about. If we find that link, I bet we solve this sucker."

Rocco stared at me across the counter. It was a very nice stare. "You know, you remind me of someone I used to watch on television when I was younger."

If he says Marcia Brady, I thought to myself, I'm dumping this Cool Whip on his head. "Who's that?"

"Jessica Fletcher."

"Jessica Fletcher?" I said, not sure if I should be flattered. "The old lady who wrote mysteries? The one Angela Lansbury played?"

"Yeah," he replied. "You're like Jessica Fletcher. Only a lot younger and with a much better rack."

Now this was talk a woman could learn to love. "Jessica Fletcher but with better tits?" I repeated.

"Yeah," he laughed.

"Or how about Nancy Drew, but with a vagina?"

"How about it," said Rocco as he reached across the counter and pulled my head towards his. It was another depth bomb, one of his huge French kisses that made me think I was all the way back in high school. What seemed like eight hours later, we broke the kiss.

"I've never seen your bedroom," he said.

"Right this way." I grabbed his hand. I felt like I was a kid and it was Christmas morning.

"I might need to shower," he said as we went up the stairs.

"I've got one of those as well," I said as I kissed him. This time I provided the depth bomb.

145

Rocco's shower provided me with just enough time to find a black silk teddy from Victoria's Secret that I hadn't worn in over two years. Fortunately, the lingerie gods had been merciful: it still hung beautifully on me. I was stretching out on the bed when he came into the room, still wet, a towel wrapped around his waist. He noticed my teddy.

"That looks nice."

I gestured to his towel. "So does that. Never looked better as a matter of fact." A single pearl of water rolled down his pecs, over his nipple and into his six pack, where it evaporated from the heat in the region.

"Maybe I should take it off," he said with a grin as he walked over to the bed.

"Maybe you should."

He did.

I've got to pause here because that's what I did in real life. And then I started to talk.

"Oh my God!" I said.

Rocco blushed. First time I'd ever seen him to do that.

"Oh my God!" I couldn't help repeating myself.

He leaned over and kissed me. "Don't worry. I'm not going to hurt you," he whispered in my ear. And then his hands were on me, big loving hands that caressed me, massaged me, made me forget all about that third leg of his. I started to sink happily into eternity with him.

* * * *

Much faster than I'd anticipated, I returned to real time.

"Well," I said, "too bad I didn't put on a two minute egg. We could be eating by now."

Rocco trailed his hand down my back and drew a small, lazy circle right above my coccyx. "I get very excited the first time I'm with a woman," he said. "But the good thing is, I can go again right away."

I took a look. He wasn't lying.

And this time, he took his time. An hour later I was lying in his arms and he was drawing that circle on my lower back again. "Was that better?"

I arched my back as he kept drawing. "Much."

He kissed the top of my head. "And this time, no interruptions."

"I'm still trying to explain that to Max."

"He's upset with you?"

I snuggled closer to him. As I get older, I like the snuggling even more than curtain raiser. "No. He'd just rather not think of his mom being with a man. You must know about that."

"I guess."

"You guess? You didn't go through the whole thing about being sexually active and not talking to your parents about it? Come on."

"I guess."

I pulled my head up and looked at him. He looked as good as ever. "You know all about me. That I'm a novelist, that I used to be an actress. You've met my son. I don't know anything about you."

He trailed his finger back up my spine and rubbed the back of my neck. "What do you want to know?"

I moved my head back to increase the friction of his hand on my flesh. "Well, when did you become a cop?"

"Five years ago."

"And before that?"

He moved his hand under my chin so that we were looking directly into each other's eyes. "You really want to know?"

"Of course I do. I've just made love with you." But of course, I didn't want to hear anything bad. Nobody wants to her they've just had sex with a serial killer.

"I told you. I made some movies." I kept looking at him. "Remember what I said about it?"

I flipped back to our conversation at the In and Out Burger. "You said it... it was a..."

He let go of my chin. "I said it was a long story."

"You made..."

He nodded. "Pornos."

Okay, this wasn't a serial killer. But it was a shock. "You were a porn star?"

He nodded.

"And then you became a cop?"

He nodded again.

I laughed out loud. I had to. It was too ridiculous. "How in the hell did you manage that transition?"

He sat up in bed and pulled me next to him. "Look, I was a young, dumb kid. I had just gotten out of the service, after a six month tour of Iraq. I didn't feel like doing anything except drinking beer and riding a motorcycle. Only motorcycles cost money and I didn't have any. A buddy of mine in the valley had been doing some pornos. He told me I could make up to a thousand a film, so I went for an interview."

"And passed with flying colors, I presume." I punched him in the arm playfully.

"Like I said, it's a long story."

"That's such a corny line."

"Actually, they used it in several of my movies. All of which were pretty lame."

"What were some of the titles?"

He shrugged. "I guess the most successful one was "Long Arm of the Law." I played a cop in that one."

I giggled. "And *that* made you want to join the L.A.P.D.?"

He put his arm around me. "Not at all. We were shooting in a house in Hidden Hills and there was some sort of problem with the owner and the rent. The entire crew got hauled into the local police station and booked for trespassing. I sat in a chair in that station for four and a half hours. I was in my late twenties and had nothing to show for it except for some good times and a bunch of porno films. And I had just met Dorothy, the musical comedy professor I told you about. They were booking us one by one, and I looked up at the bulletin board and saw a recruiting poster for the L.A.P.D. I called the next day."

"And they don't know?"

"The few who do don't care. I mean, come on, everybody's got a past. It wasn't a great thing to do, but I didn't hurt anybody. And now I'm helping people."

I put my arms around him. "That's nice."

Rocco stoked my hair as I held him. "After all, it's not as if I'm a crooked cop or anything."

"Oh no," I murmured, thinking of us just minutes before. "You're not crooked at all."

20

When I started dating musicians back in the eighties, there seemed to be one record they all loved: *Dusty in Memphis*. The album, a series of pop ballads sung R&B style by British rock star Dusty Springfield backed by an elite group of soul musicians, was actually recorded in the late sixties. But like some other wildly popular things we now take for granted—the movie version of *The Wizard of Oz*, buffalo wings, safe sex—it took awhile to catch on. By the eighties it was hard to find an L.A. musician who didn't consider *Dusty in Memphis* to be one of the greatest albums of all time.

Why am I telling you this? Because the album starts off with a song called *Just a Little Loving*. In a throaty, bedroom voice that lets you know what she's just finished doing, Dusty warbles, "Just a little loving/early in the morning/Beats a cup of coffee/for starting off the day." Truer words have never been sung.

So I was delighted when Rocco shook me gently at five in the morning and offered me another example of the skills that had led to his adult film career. This time it was sweeter, softer, even more intimate. I whined "Awww," when he crawled out of bed and started to get dressed.

"Hey, I gotta go," he said. "My shift starts at six."

"But I need some protection," I murmured.

"From what?" He leaned over and kissed me.

I sat up slowly and tried to shake the sleep from my head. "I'm serious. Last night I was threatened at a party by Sal Bucatti. And the night before that I almost had a run-in with that bouncer who got busted at No Exit. The one who was booked for assaulting Chloe Osmond."

"Sal Bucatti is mostly hot air. He usually plays by the rules. As for the bouncer, I'll check him out when I get to the station."

"You're going dressed like that?" He was in his Aerosmith T-shirt and jeans from last night.

"I keep a suit in my locker. I'll call you later, promise."

As much as I agreed with Dusty—morning lovin' beats coffee any time—I was up, so I put on a pot and started writing. I'd been away from *Malibu Bad Boy* too long; now was the time to make up for it. The French roast and Rocco's special brand of morning magic did the trick for me. By ten I was steaming away on the computer working on the very last page:

"He held her tenderly, looking down at her perfect Semitic features, her swelling breasts and the Star of David that hung between them. He thought grimly of the anti-Israeli views he had once held, of the Holocaust denial newsletter he had once funded. He buried his head in her breasts.

"Oh darling," he sobbed. "I've built such a wall of hate in my heart."

"Don't worry," she murmured. "Our love is a lethal weapon."

Done! 547 pages of Hollywood, Holocaust, and hot, hot, sex. And every single word of it fiction, mind you. Had Hemingway ever felt this good? Had Willa Cather? Well, perhaps they had, since they wrote better stuff than I did. But I was one happy lady as I reached for the phone and dialed Lynn in New York.

"Hello my dear editor."

"Nikki, love, how are you?"

"I'm fantastic. I just finished the book."

"Oh my Lord!" burbled Lynn. "This is wonderful. When can I see it?"

"I'm expecting Madison any moment now. I want her to take a look at it, then she'll send it to you via electronic mail."

"Lovely. You know, Nikki, I was just thinking about you."

"Lynn, I told you I'd get the book finished, murder or no murder."

"It's not that, love. I heard from Lev Strasser today."

"Hope he didn't send you another gift basket from Dean and DeLucca," I replied, thinking back to how he and Wendy had tried to force my hand about mentioning "Revenge of the Trophy Wives" to Lynn.

"No, it was nothing like that. He wants to know if we'd like to publish a book about Luna, this new religion he's representing."

It figured that Lev would take on Luna as a client. He always had his ear to the ground for the latest thing, the newest way to make money. And besides, wasn't he on their board of directors?

"He says that Vance Packer and Laci Stivers are committed to marketing the book once it's written," Lynn continued. "You know, that could get us on Oprah." She didn't have to say anymore. Oprah Winfrey is to book sales what gin is to a good martini: the essential ingredient.

"Are you going to go for it?" I asked.

"I thought I'd discuss it with you. You're out there, you must have a sense of how big this Luna thing is. Lev mentioned that you and Vance knew each other. He even hinted you might want to write an introduction for the book."

Was that why Vance had been cozying up to me at the *Fool's Goldfish* premiere? And here all along I'd thought it was my natural irresistibility. "Lynn, the only book I've ever written the intro for was *Psychotic Vomit*, Tyler's memoir. I really don't want to do it again."

"Okay. But what do you think of the book's chances?"

"After *The Secret*, who knows? You could probably publish Dr. Phil's shopping list and sell some copies. What about that history of erectile dysfunction in colonial America that you told me about last time? There's a book I want to see."

"Oh that," Lynn said flatly. "We had to abandon it. We got a cease and desist letter from the family of Alexander Hamilton. Turns out he could get it up after all."

Just as I was hanging up, Madison came in the room.

"I've got news you won't believe," I said to her, knowing she would never figure me for having finished the book.

"I've got news *you* won't believe," she replied.

"Okay," I said. "You first. But I bet I got you beat."

She held up a silver computer disk. "We just got this in at *TMZ*. It's a sex tape of Stavos Nikros with a bunch of women, including Wendy Strasser and Rita Collins."

"You win!" I gasped as Madison walked over to the computer and popped it in. For some reason, the sound came on before the picture. A woman was panting, and in between pants, she was talking. "Don't. Ever. Stop!" Then the picture appeared, a pretty good picture with a dateline beneath it that read Feb. 17, 2011, 3:12 PM. Like you'd really notice the dateline when the picture was of Stavos pounding away at a middle-aged blond. You could see her face, but only his butt. Still, you couldn't mistake him.

"It must be a hidden camera or a security tape," I said to Madison. "It's not moving."

She nodded her head. "And it's perfectly positioned to record the woman's face. Do you know who she is?"

"Oh. Baby. Yes!" the woman on the tape was screaming. Despite all the grimacing, it was easy to make out her face.

"Yes, I do," I said. "That's Warren Leuup's ex-wife, Rebecca. She used to show up sometimes at the Polo Lounge for lunch. Until Leuup divorced her, that is. I heard he got all the money and she moved to Scottsdale."

"Bring! It! Home!" howled the ex-Mrs. Leuup.

"Looks like she's having fun," said Madison.

"Especially for a gal her age." Rebecca was easily in her fifties; after all, she had been Leuup's first, and, to date, only wife. I recognized the terra cotta walls and the single votive candle: I'd gotten my massage in the same room.

"Madison," I asked gulping, "am I on this tape? Because, I got a massage from Stavos the other day myself."

She shook her head. "But wait till you see these." She fiddled with the keyboard, advanced the disc, and suddenly Rita Collins appeared on the screen. Instead of Rebecca Leuup's panting, Rita moaned softly like a lost child. "Oh my darling," she whimpered as she wrapped her arms around Stavos' back and pull him closer to her.

I felt like a voyeur watching Rita at such a vulnerable moment. "Can we stop?" I asked Madison.

"You don't want to see Wendy?"

That wouldn't bother me. "Go ahead." Madison advanced the disc again and there was Wendy, in high heels, her legs hooked around Stavos, pulling him deeper into her with each thrust. "Come on cowboy," she growled as she reached back and smacked his ass. The dateline on the bottom of the image read April 7, 2011, 11:35 AM. That was several months after the scene with Rita.

"Where the hell did you get this thing?"

"This isn't the original. It's a dupe I burned so you could see it."

"But how did *TMZ* get ahold of it?"

"That's why I knew you'd want to see it. Chloe Osmond is trying to sell it to us. She wants one hundred thousand dollars for it."

I was thunderstruck, a favorite word of mine that I rarely get to use. I sank down on the sofa, Madison beside me. "I've got to call Rita," I said, grabbing the phone. She picked up on the third ring.

"Rita, it's Nikki. I have some big news."

"What is it?" Her voice sounded weak and distant.

"There's a sex tape I've just seen. It's Stavos Nikros with a bunch of different women. And you're one of them."

She hung up on me instantly. And I thought I'd been doing her favor. But maybe not.

"She already knew?" asked Madison.

"I think so. Otherwise, why hang up? I mean, you'd want to know the details if someone called you up and said they'd just seen you screwing, right?"

Madison nodded.

"Something's going on here. Rita's been acting strange for some time now. She's always weepy and upset. I thought it was because Stavos dumped her, but now I think there's something more."

"You think it's because she knew about the tape?"

"At least that. Whenever we get together she makes comments about how poor she is. Beverly told me she got shafted in the divorce."

"Palmer didn't have to pay out that much?" asked Madison.

"Apparently not." I reached out and hit play on the computer. There was Rita again, moaning and grinding under Stavos. "And this must be the reason. I'll bet you Palmer has seen this. He probably used it against her in the proceedings. Hell, for all we know he could have paid to have it made."

Madison's eyes widened. "A follow up to *Thunder over Bethlehem*?"

"Or a way to keep all the profits from it," I said as I jumped to another spot on the disc. Now Wendy Strasser and Stavos were going at it. I tapped the keyboard again and we were back to Rebecca Leuup.

"Look at this, three women who got divorced…"

"Wendy Strasser got divorced?" Madison looked surprised.

"She was going to," I continued. "Or, to put it more accurately, Lev was planning to dump her. Like Palmer dumped Rita and like Warren Leuup dumped Rebecca. What a great deal for these guys. They show up at the divorce hearing with a copy of a tape of their wife screwing her masseur. Probably saves them a lot of money."

Madison whistled softly. "So why is Chloe Osmond trying to sell us this tape?"

"Elementary, my dear Madison," I said, as I thought back to my lunch of a week ago at the Polo Lounge with Joel and Chloe. "She needed money to keep her boutique going. She was getting into debt and getting desperate."

"Her dad wouldn't give it to her?"

I shook my head. "Joel was trying to be the good parent, teach her some responsibility."

"Everything's beginning to fit together," said Madison. "It's all so cozy."

"This is no cozy," I replied as I settled back on the sofa, plumping the pillow behind me. "Cozies are for those ladies who write the books with the recipes in them. This is a nasty Beverly Hills murder case with blackmail and theft, maybe even extortion. Do you know how Chloe got the disc?"

Madison shook her head. "She didn't actually speak to anyone at the station. She approached a paparazzi and asked him to play middle man for her. In fact, she did it the other night at No Exit."

"When she had that big dust-up with that lousy bouncer, Mr. Meatball?"

"Yep. The photographer came to our offices the next day and relayed the offer. She brought the disc in this morning."

I pulled it out of the computer. "And you snuck this copy out for me?"

She smiled guiltily. "I knew you'd want to see it."

I leaned over and gave her a hug. "Your secret's safe. I love you for doing this."

"But, I guess we still don't know where Chloe got this disc from."

"I bet she stole it," I said.

"From Stavos?"

"Maybe. They're supposed to be friends. But this tape isn't that valuable to him."

"Are you kidding?' said Madison. "A sex tape like this could turn him into a national name. That was Chloe's pitch to us, that it was Laci Stivers's boyfriend having sex with all the wives of Beverly Hills. If this thing hits the air, he could be as big as Tommy Lee."

"Oh come now, Madison, few people are as big as Tommy Lee." I thought fondly of Rocco and our night together. "Is *TMZ* going to post this?"

She shrugged. "The word is the lawyers are scared to death by it, mainly because Palmer Collins' ex-wife is on it. They think he might make trouble because the tape makes him look bad."

That didn't make sense to me. "Why would he care what how his ex-wife looks? He couldn't wait to dump her."

"You think Chloe got the tape from him?"

"I can't see Palmer bothering with her."

"Bothering?" Madison was mystified.

I thought back to another conversation with Joel, the one I'd had with him just two nights ago at the premiere of *Fool's Goldfish* when he told me Chloe was dating an older man.

"Chloe was having an affair with an older man. Joel told me. And I'm betting it was either Lev Strasser or Warren Leuup. That's probably how she got the tape. She lifted it from one of them."

"Which one?"

Who would be more likely to get involved with Chloe? "Let's see," I said reaching for the phone. I dialed information. "I'd like the number for Chlothes Boutique on Robertson and when you get it can you connect me?"

"Certainly," replied the operator. A few seconds later the call went through.

"Chlothes," said Chloe.

I was in luck.

"May I help you?"

I lowered my voice to an executive secretary growl. "Please hold for Warren Leuup."

There was a pause, and then Chloe hung up. Just like Rita had.

"We've got our answer," I said to Madison as I put down the phone. The moment I did, it rang again. It was so quick I almost screamed.

"Hello"

"Hey, it's me." It was Rocco. I felt slightly self-conscious talking to him with Madison in the room.

"How have you been, Detective?"

"Skip the formal stuff," he said. "I've got a sex tape down here you've got to look at. That boyfriend of Laci Stivers is screwing a bunch of your girlfriends."

21

The West L.A. Police Station, the place where the investigation of the O.J. Simpson case was launched, could use a good paint job. Something in a salmon to offset all the dull brown. After that, some new blinds and more comfortable upholstery wouldn't hurt. Your sense of Hollywood glamour evaporates the moment you step into the building. No wonder all the actors look so drab in their DUI mug shots.

"I didn't invite you here to play Martha Stewart," said Rocco when I told him all this. "Just follow me."

"Yes, Detective," I said with a smile. We stepped into a small elevator and descended to the basement. On the way down, he gave my hand a nice, tight squeeze. By then we had arrived at the evidence room. We were met by a stout, white-haired old Irish cop who looked like he had been left over from the last revival of *Dragnet*.

"Hey Roc," he said when he saw us coming.

"Hey Duff," replied my hero. "I've got to check the Anthony Salazar stuff again."

"You know where it is." He buzzed us in and returned to his paperback book. Sadly, it wasn't one of mine.

"This is the Anthony Salazar who was the bouncer at No Exit?" I asked

"The very one," he said as the wire mesh door clanked closed behind us.

I followed Rocco down two long aisles filled with cardboard boxes of all sizes. The warehouse sized room had wooden crates stacked against almost every inch of wall space. This was the garage sale of your nightmares. Rocco reached into one of the shelves and pulled a laptop out of a large box that had a sticker reading "Salazar, Anthony" slapped on it.

"He had an outstanding warrant for weapons possession. Two of the guys in the department busted him at his store three weeks ago."

"What kind of store does he have?" I asked. I couldn't picture Salazar running a boutique on Rodeo.

"A pizza joint, what else?"

Well, that explained the garlic scent on his knuckles the other night.

Rocco slid the laptop onto a nearby table and turned it on. "They impounded this as evidence and Salazar hasn't gotten around to submitting a request for its return." He scrolled down the menu and hit play. "Look at this."

It was the same tape Madison had shown me an hour earlier. After what Rocco had said on the phone I wasn't surprised, but I was mystified. How the hell had a bouncer at a Sunset Strip nightclub gotten a hold of what I had now come to think of as "the Stavos sex tape?"

"Well that's a real good question," said Rocco. "I think we ought to get ourselves a couple slices and ask him."

* * * *

Tony's Pizza was located at the far end of Hollywood Boulevard, near Cahuenga, lodged between a store that sold T-shirts, apparently only of Michael Jackson, and a windowless store front that offered a "relaxing Thai massage" to those who ventured inside. "Hollywood's Best Pizza" was stenciled on the front window of the shop in large red letters. Salazar was behind the counter when we walked in.

"Anthony Salazar?" asked Rocco.

"He's in Hawaii," he said as wiped some flour off the marble top in front of him. "Can I give him a message?"

"Yeah," replied Rocco. "You can tell him his computer's still down at the L.A. West Police Station. Only it's been impounded. For having underage porn on it."

Salazar didn't blink. "There's nothing underage on that computer."

"Then you ought to stop by and pick it up, Mr. Salazar."

He looked over at me, the barest flicker of interest passing over his thick, sluggish features as he seemed to recognize me from the other night at No Exit. Guess it really hadn't been that good a disguise. "What the hell are you doing here?"

"I came to taste Hollywood's Best Pizza," I said.

"Don't believe what you read," he grunted.

Rocco leaned over the counter. "We've got to talk, Mr. Salazar."

"Talk to my lawyer," he said as he wiped the flour off his hands with a dish towel.

Rocco leaned in even closer. "I'd rather talk to you." He reached over the counter and dipped his hand in an aluminum bowl full of red sauce. Then he pulled his hand back and flung the sauce towards the ceiling. It spattered all over a security camera mounted on the wall; red sauce covered the lens.

"What the hell!" Salazar growled.

Rocco was too quick for him. He was behind the counter before the bum had a chance to move and grabbed his arm. "This is police brutality!" wailed Salazar.

"Not really," said Rocco. "This is." And he pushed Salazar's arm behind his back and up towards his shoulders until the big baby started to wail.

I felt like I was back on the playground in 5th grade.

Rocco pulled out a pair of handcuffs, snapped one of them on Salazar's wrist and the other on the silver handle of the pizza oven. When Salazar tried to break free, the oven door just flew open emitting a blast of heat.

Rocco folded his arms and leaned back on the marble top. "Feel like talking now?"

Sweat began to bead on Salazar's brow. Apparently it took a great deal of heat to bake Hollywood's best pizza. "About what?" he sneered.

"About the porn tape on your computer. The one we've got at the station.'

"This is illegal!" Salazar waved his hand up and down, causing the oven door to bang open and close.

"I'll bet the story behind that tape is illegal too," countered Rocco.

"You'll never know," shrugged Salazar.

Rocco looked over the marble top and then reached for the pizza slicer that was lying on it. It was one of those silver circles, held in place by a handle, and studded with jagged teeth. Rocco grabbed Salazar's free hand and slammed it on to the marble top.

"Hey!"

Rocco jammed the pizza slicer between Salazar's two fingers. He rolled it up, pushing on the flesh between the fingers, drawing blood instantly.

"Jesus!" Salazar howled in pain.

Rocco pushed down harder on the cutter.

"Aggghhhhh!"

He pushed down even harder.

I looked away. This was too much for me.

"Stop!" Salazar was in tears.

Rocco dropped the pizza slicer. He looked at Salazar calmly. "Tell me how you got the tape."

"From a friend," grunted Salazar

Rocco scooped up another handful of red sauce and flung it in Salazar's face. "Not good enough."

"Rocco," I said. This was getting ugly; he was getting ugly. I hadn't expected this. He just looked over at me, a simple stare. It said, "This is my territory; if you don't like it you can leave."

Well, I wasn't leaving.

"Who gave you the tape," Rocco repeated.

"Sal Bucatti," muttered Salazar. Between the sweat and the red sauce, he was a mess.

"You work for him?"

"I know him."

"Why did he give you the tape?"

Salazar shrugged. "Who the hell knows? For safekeeping."

"Where did he get it from?"

"That's the kind of question I don't ask," Salazar replied. You had to believe him.

But that left me with a question. "Did you give this tape to Chloe Osmond?"

Salazar made an ugly face, an uglier one than he normally wore. "That stupid little broad? She stole the tape, for Christ's sake!"

"From who?" I asked.

"How the hell would I know? I never saw her before the other night."

It was beginning to fit together. "That's why you were at No Exit? To get the tape?"

He shrugged, but you could tell it was a yes.

"How'd you know she had the tape?" asked Rocco.

"Bucatti knew," he replied. "She'd been contacting people, trying to sell it. He wanted me to get it back."

"And give it back to who?" I asked.

"That's another of those questions I don't ask. He just wanted the tape in his possession."

"Was he blackmailing people with the tape?" Rocco asked.

Salazar didn't respond: he looked away. On the marble top, a fly lazily circled a pile of fresh pizza dough, contemplating a landing.

Rocco picked up the pizza slicer and rolled it over the dough. That spooked the fly and Salazar. "You've got an outstanding warrant for weapon possession, and two nights ago you were booked for assault. You really want to play games?"

Salazar was silent.

159

So was Rocco. But he didn't put the slicer down.

"I don't know much," Salazar finally said.

"Just tell us what you know," I said. Rocco shot me an amused glance. It said: *Hello, Lady Cop.*

"They hired Sal to act as an advisor to Luna," he began. "Someone who could step in… when they had a problem."

"Vance Packer?" I asked.

Salazar nodded. "He wanted somebody who could manage things, keep bad news out of the papers, make sure things happened right. Like I said, an advisor."

Rocco smiled grimly. He was thinking the same thing I was: this wasn't advising, it was enforcing, in the style of Don Corleone and Tony Soprano. "Where does the sex tape come in?" asked Rocco.

"The guy was making them," replied Salazar.

"The guy?" said Rocco.

"The beauty boy, the one who gives massages."

"And blackmailing the women with them?" I asked.

Salazar shook his head. "It wasn't even his idea. It was his girlfriend's."

"Laci Stivers?" That surprised me.

"That's her. The bimbo with all the money and no brains. She thought it would be a hot idea to make these sex tapes of her boyfriend screwing all these women who were his clients."

"For kicks?" asked Rocco.

"No."

"Well you said it wasn't blackmail, so it wasn't for cash."

"It was for cash," said Salazar, smiling grimly. "Only not the way you think it was. They would videotape him screwing the women, then give the tape to the husband so he could use it in the divorce settlement and make his wife settle for millions of dollars less than she wanted."

"Why would Laci Stivers do all this for Luna and Vance Packer?" asked Rocco.

"Because he sponsored her stupid TV show and she wanted to stay on the air. It was her way of paying Packer off," Salazar replied.

"Vance used the tapes to get the husbands to sign up for Luna?" I asked.

Salazar nodded. "They gave lots of money too."

I turned to Rocco. "Now we know how the Collins Center got financed for Luna. Rita Collins' alimony built that place."

I turned back to Salazar. "And Chloe knew of these tapes because she hung around with Laci and Stavos?"

"Yeah, but that's not where she got the tape. According to them."

Right, I thought to myself. After all, hadn't I heard the receptionist at Stavos' spa telling him there was a "problem with one of the tapes?" Now I knew what the problem was. And I was willing to bet my phone call had proven where the tape came from: Warren Leuup.

"What do you know about Warren Leuup?" I asked Salazar.

"Good person to get a divorce from," he replied.

"Was he seeing Chloe Osmond?" I pressed

"I told you. I saw her for the first time at No Exit."

"Where you assaulted her," said Rocco.

"What do you want me to say?" he shrugged. "Sal wanted the tape back."

I wanted to clear up the stuff with Leuup. "So Leuup's connection to Luna was that he saved on his wife's divorce thanks to the sex tape?"

"He was the first one, from what I heard," said Salazar.

I looked at Rocco. "And the others, Palmer and Lev, Leuup probably recruited them."

"It's extortion," he said calmly. "Using the tapes to get them to give money to Luna. Extortion, plain and simple."

"Even if the men used the tapes first to get their wives to settle for smaller alimony payments?" I asked. "I mean, the tapes were a benefit to Leuup and Palmer and Lev. They saved them millions."

"That'll be up to the D.A.," replied Rocco. "But if you're using extraordinary means to get money out of people, it can be extortion. Bucatti and Vance Packer can both be indicted for this."

"You'll never make it stick," sneered Salazar.

"Of course I will,' snapped Rocco, "with you as a star witness repeating what you just told me. Unless you want to do five to seven on the combined weapons and assault charges."

"Hey," protested Salazar, "I'm a first offender."

"Yeah," said Rocco. "And Roman Polanski likes older women." He uncuffed Salazar's hand from the oven handle and threw a dish towel at him. "Clean yourself up. You're a mess."

"Let's get out of here," he said to me.

"Where are we going?"

"I'm going to visit Sal Bucatti at his office in Beverly Hills and you're going to go home."

161

22

The weird thing was I actually did go home. I didn't want to, of course. I wanted to stay with Rocco and see what happened when he visited Bucatti's office. But I realized that this was building very quickly to something—maybe something very nasty. The sex tape had blown the lid off all the pretending that people like Rita and Palmer Collins and Lev Strasser had been doing. And then there was Chloe and Laci and Stavos and Vance Packer and whatever their involvement was. This tape had been used against people, and now it was probably going public.

So while I was disappointed that I might miss the big bang-up ending, I was kind of relieved to be headed home. Plus, it was nice to know that Rocco felt protective of me. I felt pretty good as I turned off Sunset and headed to my old stomping grounds, Casa Tyler.

That was before I saw Chloe sitting in her car across from my house. The good feelings vanished as quickly as Angelina Jolie when she saw Jennifer Aniston approaching on the red carpet.

I turned my head the other way, like I was looking at my neighbor's front yard, and kept driving. That ought to be inconspicuous, I said to myself. Of course, not everyone in Beverly Hills drives a gold Bentley. *Could be a big give away* I thought as I pressed down on the gas pedal.

I'd been so clever calling Chloe and pretending I was Warren Leuup. She'd been just as clever, she must have hit Star 69 to see who was calling and up came my number.

Well, that left me with only one place to go: Warren Leuup's office. I was convinced that was where the tape came from and I wanted to confirm it. Plus I had a plan.

"Are you calling about lunch?" asked Inez when I reached her at the switchboard of Leuup and Spangler. "Already? Usually people wait about six months out here to follow up on that."

I told her what I wanted to do and there was a long pause on the other end of the line.

"He's not here today," she said.

"Perfect," I replied as I headed down Santa Monica Boulevard to Century City.

"He's at the Collins Center for a meeting on Luna."

"Even better," I said. "Then you'll do this for me? You'll sneak me into his office?"

That led to a *really* long pause.

"Bring a tape measure with you," said Inez. "We'll pass you off as a decorator."

Then I called Rocco and told him where I was headed.

"What the hell are you doing?" he fumed. "I told you to go home."

"I can't," I wailed. "Chloe Osmond is sitting outside my house, waiting for me. I don't know what the hell she's up to, or what she might do. Besides, Warren Leuup isn't even in his office. There's no risk. And I bet I find a copy of the sex tape. I'm cracking this case wide open for you!"

"Damn it!' he said. "I'm practically at Bucatti's office now. I'm pulling into the garage. I want you to—" And of course, that's when I lost him, because everyone knows you can't keep a cellphone connection going in a parking garage. I mean Rocco's a big, bad detective, he should know that.

Ten minutes later, having literally flung the keys to my Bentley at the valet parker at the 1350 Avenue of the Stars building, I was being ushering into Warren Leuup's office by Inez. "If anyone comes in, you're on your own." She closed the door behind her and I went over to Leuup's computer. It was sitting on his desk and it was on.

This, of course, was the moment. I wished I'd asked Max about his computer and all the things he'd learned to do with it: hacking, getting into people's files, the various applications, all that good stuff. But I did know enough to call up Leuup's documents and start scrolling through them. There were endless entries marked "Litigant" or "Proposal;" I wasn't going to waste my time trying to open any of them.

I concentrated on where I would hide a sex file if I kept one on my computer. Under my spouse's name? There was nothing labeled Rebecca in the file. My kid's name? Leuup and Rebecca didn't have any kids. So I scrolled down to Luna and began to open the documents that had it as part of their name. There was a building permit for the Collins Center, a monthly bill for legal services, a letter to a contractor regarding late installment of lighting fixtures in the Center. I was getting nowhere fast, but I kept opening the documents one after the other, convinced I was going in the right direction. Which was probably why I didn't hear Inez when she reentered the room.

"We've got company," she said.

I looked up to see her walking into the room, holding her hands in front of her, which looked odd. But then I saw Chloe walking behind her. And Chloe had a gun in her hand. I actually gasped when I saw her.

She looked hard and mean, scarier than I'd ever seen her look before. Her clothes were a mess and she had that same Jesse Kamm scarf wrapped around her head. "Where's the tape?" she said.

"I was just looking for it here," I replied, gesturing to the computer.

"Bullshit," said Chloe. "Your assistant stole a copy from *TMZ* this morning. And I want it back.'

There was an edge of desperation to her voice that told me I had to tread very lightly. "Chloe, I'm surprised you're here. How did you even know that I—"

"I followed you," she snapped.

Well, why not? The Bentley wasn't inconspicuous; I guess I hadn't managed to lose her in the midday traffic.

"Why don't you put that down?" said Inez cautiously as she looked at the gun in Chloe's hand. It was a big gun, silver and shiny, and Chloe held it awkwardly.

"I want that tape!" She thrust the gun forward, almost as if she was going to fire it.

I gave out a little shriek.

"Chloe! Please!" I said. "You don't want to hurt anyone."

"Why not put the gun down?" repeated Inez.

"Yeah, put it down, you stupid bitch."

It was Laci Stivers. She had materialized in the open doorway behind Chloe. Laci had dressed down: an oversized Armani T-shirt, red tights and a pair of Chanel boots. And she was holding a gun, just like Chloe. Hers was smaller, and picked up the light a lot better. A fashion revolver, I guessed.

"Laci!" gasped Chloe.

Laci gestured towards Chloe's gun with her gun. "Put that down."

And just like that, Chloe put her gun down on the coffee table. She always had been the ugly duckling in their relationship. When it came time for Laci to play her card, Chloe just folded. Story of her life.

Laci's face was shiny and immobile as ever, but her eyes radiated pure hatred. "Now get me that tape, bitch."

"How did you know I was here?" gulped Chloe.

"I followed you, bitch," hissed Laci.

Well, it must have been quite a motorcade down Santa Monica Boulevard, I thought to myself. "Now get me that tape. It's mine."

"It is not," Chloe protested. "I stole it. It's mine." The logic of the Beverly Hills brat.

"I stole it from Warren," continued Chloe. "It's mine." So I had been right about their affair. That felt good.

"You screwed that old man?" sneered Laci. "God, you're so pathetic."

"Not as pathetic as you," spat back Chloe. "Having your boyfriend screw every old woman in Beverly Hills so you could be a TV star."

Okay, I thought to myself, we can start taping *The Young and the Restless* any time now.

"Why don't you put the gun down?" said Inez to Laci, repeating her very good idea.

"Shut up," Laci snarled back, waving the tiny gun at her. "You don't get to tell me what to do."

"The lady told you to put the gun down."

It was Sal Bucatti, and he was holding a serious gun in his hand. A big, thick black gun with a chamber that looked heavier than Chloe and Laci put together.

"Who the fu—" But the words died on her lips when Laci turned and saw who was behind her. She put her gun down on the coffee table, next to Chloe's. She was a very stupid girl, but she wasn't dumb. I wondered if either of the guns was a Ruger, the type of gun that had killed Tamara and Wendy.

Sal looked over at me. "How's it going, Nikki?" This time he didn't slip a piece of candy in my hand.

"Did you follow Laci and Chloe here?" I managed to ask, my heartbeat growing quicker by the second.

"I'm here on behalf of a client who wants his interests protected," he replied smoothly. Years of dealing with slick Hollywood lawyers had obviously rubbed off on Sal.

"And why are you here?" he continued, looking at me, his gun, like Laci's and Chloe's before it, pointed directly at me. "You came here for legal advice? Or perhaps you're trying to discover who's involved in the theft of a certain tape?"

"You're answering your own questions," I said.

"I got a lot of questions," he replied. "Why don't we all go down to the Collins Center and I can start asking them."

Laci, Chloe, and even Inez looked positively fear-struck in the face of this legendary sleaze. I'm not saying that I felt full of courage, but I hated the bastard, hated him for what he did to that little goldfish, and didn't feel like going without a fight.

"You'll never get away with this," I said.

165

He chuckled. "If you wrote stuff that dumb in your books, you'd never sell." He gestured with his gun towards the doorway. "Now come on."

As we started to edge out of the office, Bucatti reached out, grabbed the scarf off Chloe's head and draped it over his hand, rendering the gun invisible. "And no funny stuff," he added as we made our way down the office corridor. The two legal secretaries who were at their desks never looked up.

"Push the button," he said to Inez when we reached the reception area where the elevators were located.

She did, just as Laci began to tap the sole of her Chanel boot impatiently on the marble floor.

"Something wrong, girly?" inquired Bucatti. Laci stopped tapping. Chloe didn't look hard and mean anymore; she looked scared to death.

Bucatti brushed the muzzle of the revolver against my back while we waited for the elevator, as if I were likely to forget that I was with a well-known thug who was carrying a deadly weapon. Then the bell rang, the doors opened, and we all stepped into the elevator, Bucatti last. The four of us huddled together on the right side of the car. Over on the left was a thin blond woman, but I was too frightened to really notice her.

I was okay until the 19th floor when the car lurched to a halt and a black man in a business suit stepped into the car. He patted his side pocket, where I guess his cell phone was supposed to be, and said "Damn. I'll take the next car." I felt queasy.

The doors closed and the car seemed to go into a kind of free fall. We parachuted down the rest of the floors in one big swoop, and I felt my stomach rising into my throat. Then there was another lurch and the car came to a shuddering halt, but the door didn't open.

That did it for me. I leaned forward and spewed vomit all over the thin blond woman.

"Oh my God!" she screamed. "Oh my God!"

I looked over to see that I had just barfed on Tori Spelling.

Bucatti was furious. The scarf had fallen from his hand and the gun was now out in the open. Then the elevator doors opened.

"Run!" screamed Inez just as she did that very thing.

"Oh my God!" repeated Tori as she dashed out of the car, still covered in my slime.

I would have looked at her, but my eyes were trained on Rocco. He had been there when the elevator doors opened, and now he was standing with his pistol drawn, pointed directly at Bucatti.

"Let's go to headquarters," Rocco said to him. Bucatti moved out of the elevator into the lobby and Chloe, Laci and I followed him. I looked over to see Tori who was still wiping the remnants of my breakfast from her outfit.

"Oh my God!' she repeated, yet again.

She looked so sad there, covered in vomit, screaming in a high rise lobby in Century City. I suddenly realized how adolescent and foolish I'd been all these years, resenting her getting a break ahead of me in the business. After all, it's who you know.

The lobby guard, who had seen all of this, came over with his pistol drawn. Bucatti dropped his gun on the marble floor and raised his hands.

Stuck without a screenwriter, Tori repeated, "Oh my God!"

"Are you okay?" Rocco said to me.

I had wiped my lips with a tissue and recovered from the elevator ride. "I'm fine," I replied. "Thanks for asking." I was filled with a good feeling for Rocco, for how he'd been there for me. And for Tori, who I felt I'd finally made peace with. How silly of me to have blamed her for my misdirected acting career.

"Oh my God!" Meryl Streep couldn't have said it any better.

Rocco put his arm around me as the security guard marched Bucatti to the door. Chloe and Laci followed in mute amazement. "Let's get you out of here," he said softly. We started to walk to the entrance of the building, when I took one last look at a troubled face, a face I had once hated.

"Oh my God!"

"Tori," I said as we headed out the door, "I forgive you."

23

"I used to think this place could use some salmon," I said to Esme Lopez as I looked around her office at the West L.A. Police Station, "but now I'm not so sure."

"Fish is nasty," Esme replied. "My partner and I won't eat it. We won't even feed it to our cat."

Esme was the supervising officer on both Tamara and Wendy's murder cases, and I was learning that if you want to get to the bottom of a homicide, it helps to have a Latina lesbian on your side. I was killing time in Esme's office while Rocco questioned Chloe. Laci was being held while she waited for her lawyer, Stavos, and, for all I knew, her publicist. Bucatti had been booked immediately. Since he had been waving a gun in public, they charged him with attempted assault with a deadly weapon. I hadn't heard from my new pal Tori, but assumed she was okay.

Esme was shuffling through some crime photos. "Look at these." She extended two pictures, a head shot of Tamara and one of Wendy. In both, the gold hoop earring with the little brass monkey seemed to jump out at you. "Do you know why they're wearing the same damn earring?"

"I have no clue. Except that I saw Chloe Osmond wearing the very same earring, both earrings, not just one, a few days earlier at the Polo Lounge."

"You're saying these are her earrings?" asked Esme.

"I wish I knew. When I asked Chloe about them, she said they had disappeared."

Esme took the head shots back. "Well, if they are her earrings, the DNA will confirm it." She handed me two other pictures; they were of Tamara and Wendy's bodies.

"Check these out," said Esme. "They're even wearing the same damn belt. Can you figure that?"

"They both bought it at Barneys," I said. "I ran into them the day they bought them. It was right before they were both killed."

Esme looked at the pictures with me. "These outfits are terrible. They're dumb ass. The red belt buckle clashes with the blue top. Can't these Beverly Hills women even dress?"

"You're a fashonista?" I asked, not trying to hide my amusement.

"Not me,' replied Esme. "My partner. She works for Bravo. She's the fashion coordinator for all those "Real Housewives" shows. And she would never let one of her ladies look like these two."

"How did the two of you meet?"

"On a bike run. How else do you think lesbians meet?" Her laugh was deep and soulful. It washed away some of the ugliness of the afternoon. "We actually met through Rocco. I went out to the run with him, and Monique was there."

"Love at first sight?"

"Something clicked," Esme said.

"Something clicked," I repeated. "I remember how that one used to go." Esme was at least ten years younger than me.

"I saw you and Rocco when you came in," she said. "I think you remember better than you're letting on."

"You've known Rocco a long time?"

She nodded. "Been working with him for three years now."

"He seems like a nice guy," I said. We were getting into "girlfriend" talk now, and I couldn't help but love it.

"Oh he is," replied Esme. "As long as he doesn't trip over his dick."

I burst out laughing. "You know?"

She shot me a wicked grin. "Everybody knows. He just thinks it's a secret. Hell, who cares if your local cop is an ex-porno star, as long as he knows how to bang a few heads together."

I thought back to Anthony Salazar and the pizza slicer. "He knows how to do that."

Esme took one last look through the pictures. "You know something else? Those suitcases they found at the apartment where you found Wendy Strasser? They had different sized clothes in them. These Beverly Hills women have some very strange weight issues. Monique said she met me as a size fourteen; she wants me to stay a size fourteen."

"You two planning to get married?" I asked.

"Well we can't do that in this state right now, can we?" Esme replied. "Come on, let's go see what Rocco is getting out of that Osmond brat."

We walked through a maze of desks and into a small, airless room located in the back of the building. A large TV monitor sat on a table in the middle of the room; it was broadcasting a feed of Rocco interrogating Chloe. He was on one side of the table; she was on the other. Just like you see on *Law and Order*.

"Were you blackmailing Wendy Strasser with the tape?" asked Rocco.

"No," Chloe replied flatly.

"Rita Collins?"

"No."

"Did you tell either of them that you were planning to sell the tape to the media?"

"No."

"Did you kill your stepmother and Wendy Strasser?"

Chloe's voice became shrill. "No! I told you that ten minutes ago. I didn't kill either of them. And I don't know who did. Where is my father?"

"We're getting in touch with him."

"He's going to get me a lawyer."

Rocco gave her a very seductive smile, the kind I had gotten just two nights ago. "This is just a preliminary conversation we're having here, Chloe. I've been working on this case from the beginning, and yet I hardly know you. I'd like to get to know you better."

"Oh brother," muttered Esme.

"Does he use this kind of stuff a lot?" I asked her.

"You'd be surprised how often it works. Even Monique thinks he's sexy.'

"Can you tell us why both your stepmother and Wendy Strasser were found wearing the same earring?" asked Rocco.

"If I could, I'd be a cop like you," Chloe replied with a big, fake smile.

"You had a pair of the same earrings, didn't you?"

She shifted uncomfortably. "Yes."

"Where are they?"

Chloe was silent.

"Where are they?"

Even on the grainy TV image I could see a tear roll down Chloe's cheek as she shook her head softly. "No one will ever believe me."

"I'll believe you, Chloe," crooned Rocco.

"Oh brother," muttered Esme again.

"I promise I'll believe you," Rocco continued.

"This is the weird thing that no one will ever believe," said Chloe as she wiped away her tears. "Tamara came to me two days before she was killed and borrowed those earrings from me."

"And you said earlier that they disappeared, right?" said Rocco.

"I didn't want to tell anyone because it looked so bad," she continued. "And no one's going to believe what I say now. They're going to think that I killed her and killed Wendy Strasser. But Tamara borrowed those earrings from me. I swear it."

Something clicked.

I turned to Esme. "Can you tell Rocco I had to run somewhere very important?"

"Sure," she said, surprised I could tear myself away.

"I'll be back real soon," I said over my shoulder as I headed out the door.

I was at the entrance when I practically ran right into Lisa Manning and her crew.

"Hello Nikki," she said, frost hanging on every syllable.

"You're here because?" I replied. She was blocking my way, even though I was trying to move around her and her sound and camera guys.

"We're here because we heard there's been a break in the Osmond and Strasser murder cases. I thought they might be booking you." Lisa's lip was so full of botox she couldn't curl it, but I got the message.

"No such luck," I replied as I maneuvered around her crew. "They can indict me for crimes against literature, but never against humanity." I started towards the parking structure.

"Oh Nikki," continued Lisa, "I want to thank you for something."

I stopped and looked back at her. "What's that?"

"The tip you gave me about finding a certain someone in Whole Foods." And with that Lisa reached into her purse and pulled out a Little Debbie Cake and flung it at me. I ducked and it hit the glass door behind me. Splat! She pulled out another. Splat! And another. Splat! I was being bombarded by Little Debbie Cakes!

"You lying witch!" screamed Lisa as she kept the fusillade of Debbie Cakes coming.

I ducked, scrambled through the door, and headed to my car. I turned the ignition on as if Lisa and her semi-automatic Little Debbie Cake cannon were still in pursuit of me. I crossed Santa Monica Boulevard and headed towards Sunset. I knew where I was going.

Something had clicked. Somewhere in the distance…

24

I walked on to the terrace of the Polo Lounge to find several of my friends there.

Joel was by himself, glasses perched on the tip of his nose, reading *The New York Times*.

Beverly was sitting with a buff young man, feeding him spoonfuls of lobster chowder. Guess she'd found herself a gubby.

Rita was sitting alone, pushing some fava beans around her plate.

I sat down at Joel's table.

"Nikki, how nice."

"Don't get up," I replied as I placed the napkin on my lap.

"I didn't." He smiled and put away the paper. "How are you? It's a gorgeous day." He was right, there was a perfectly clear sky and sunlight touched every table on the terrace.

"I've been thinking about Tamara."

"Of course," Joel said. "I am too, every moment of the day."

"I've been thinking about why she wore Chloe's earring the day she was murdered. And I've been thinking why Wendy was wearing the same earring the day she was murdered."

Joel looked puzzled. "What do you mean?"

"It just didn't make any sense," I continued as I reached over and picked up one of the rolls from the bread basket. "Why would they both be wearing the same earring, and just one earring, on the day they were murdered? Plus, if you believe what your daughter says, and I'd like to, Tamara actually borrowed that pair of earrings from her right before she was killed."

I broke the roll in half, buttered it, and placed the halves on the bread plate in front of me. Eating could wait for now.

"The other thing, which I didn't think about until today when I spoke with an officer who's working on the case, is how poorly Tamara and Wendy were dressed. Tamara was wearing a skirt she had for years, and Wendy's boots were practically worn through. They had on these belts they had bought the day I met them at Barneys. Then the earring. And finally those blue tops that didn't match the red belt buckle at all."

"I'm mystified," Joel said furrowing his brow.

"It took me a while too," I said. "The old clothes, the new belt, the earring, the blue top. And then I got it.

"Something old, something new, something borrowed, something blue. Tamara and Wendy were going to get married. To each other. They even had their suitcases packed at the hideaway where they used to meet. There were different clothes in each suitcase. They were clearly planning to run away together."

My heart was racing as I said this, but saying it helped me to believe it. And I did believe it.

Joel looked at me across the table. I'd never seen him seem so calm before. He was Zen-like in his reserve.

"They were going to New York," he said. "They were going to get married there, come back here and work for marriage equality. I couldn't let her go, Nikki. I couldn't lose her."

"How long had they been in love?" I asked him.

"A couple of months. Wendy had been having an affair with that trashy masseur Laci Stivers hangs out with, but, according to Tamara, that began to change when they had lunch one day and she confessed to Wendy how lonely she'd been since our divorce." Joel looked around the terrace. "They had the lunch right here."

"So this was a new thing for both of them?" I asked. I thought of reaching for the roll, but this was too enthralling.

"A lot of women try a gay relationship if their marriages don't work out," Joel said. "It's not that unusual. And in this case, it really took. My damn luck."

"You were that jealous?"

"Insanely." A cruel smile flickered across his face just long enough to let me know that he'd picked the appropriate adverb.

"You know how much I loved Tamara," Joel continued. "I begged her not to divorce me. She thought she would find a new life after we split. She wound up in love with her best friend."

"Did you have it all planned out?" I asked, my fascination growing. "Did you know you were going to do it that day I had lunch here with you and Chloe?"

Joel tapped his fingers on the white linen tablecloth. "I wasn't certain, but I was leaning towards it. I found out about the affair the week before. Tamara and I had several huge arguments about it. I couldn't get her to change her mind."

"So you just killed her?"

"It's not that simple!" he protested. "We were arguing. She told me they were going to run away and get married. I lost my temper." He paused and dropped his voice. "I got my gun."

"But why did you kill Wendy?"

"I had to. She was the one person who would have known I was the murderer. Instantly. I had no choice."

"So it was one right after the other?" I asked. "You killed Tamara and then you drove over to Wendy's hideaway apartment and killed her?"

Joel nodded.

"But the apartment *was* a hideaway."

"I'd been following Tamara for weeks."

"And Chloe stealing the sex tape, you knew about that?"

He nodded again. "She told me all about it that day at lunch, right before you arrived. She said she had stolen the tape from Warren Leuup and she was going to try and sell it and use the money to keep her shop going. Unless I would give her the money, of course."

"And that's why you told me at the premiere of *Fool's Goldfish* that Chloe was seeing an older man. You wanted me to discover that she and Leuup were involved."

"You'd make a good detective," replied Joel.

"In fact," I said, "you've pretty much been leading me on since that very day at lunch. Getting me to read Tamara's book was just a ploy to get me involved"

Joel smiled.

"And you wrote Warren Leuup's name in the manuscript to send me to his office."

His smile grew larger.

"You figured that if you distracted me and everybody else with this scandal about the sex tape, no one would think to look at what might have been happening between Tamara and Wendy."

Joel fanned his hands through the air as if he were shuffling a pack of cards. "I used to be a magician, Nikki. They always tell you to create a diversion with your right hand so the audience won't notice what you're doing with your left."

I was dazzled by his ruthlessness. I'd known Joel for over two decades, and yet I'd never realized how low he was willing to go. He had been bold and ingenious and incredibly sneaky. No wonder he'd done so well in this town.

My stomach tightened as I listened to Joel's even, dispassionate tone. This psychopath had just calmly confessed to slaughtering two women, one of whom he professed to be deeply in love with. What would he think of doing to me?

Still, there was one last thing I had to say to him.

"It's quite a scheme you put together," I said in reluctant admiration. "You had just about every angle covered."

Now his smile disappeared. "Thank you."

"But there was one thing you forgot. Chloe. You left her hanging out there facing a murder charge. Your own daughter."

"I didn't forget her," he protested. "I was going to get her the best defense money could buy. O.J.'s people. I would have made it work, Nikki. Remember, I'm a producer."

I looked across the table at him, at the cold indifference I saw in his eyes.

"You're a monster."

"Oh now don't say that. We've known each other for twenty years, for God's sake."

That's when I noticed that he had a gun in his hand and it was pointed at me. I was petrified.

"Is that a Ruger?" I managed to ask.

"Yes."

"The same gun you used to kill Tamara and Wendy Strasser?" My heart was racing so fast I felt dizzy.

"Yes."

"And now you plan to kill me with it?"

"No," he replied. "I plan to kill myself with it."

Joel drew the revolver to his head and pulled the trigger. There was a loud pop and he slumped back against his chair. His jaw dropped open. A stream of blood began to flow from his temple.

Suddenly Javier was at my side.

"Oh my heavens, Mrs. Tyler!" he exclaimed. "What has happened? What can I do for you?"

I reached for the roll I'd been resisting for the entire conversation and took a bite of it.

"I'll have the McCarthy salad, Javier," I said. "Dressing on the side."

25

"**Hello** love."

It was Lynn. It was also three days, and several hundred headlines, later.

"You're the only person I haven't heard from," I mumbled, rearranging the pillows behind my head. It was seven ten in the morning.

"Well I've been busy. Reading."

"Oh, so you didn't hear what happened to me?"

There was the tiniest pause, and then the damn broke. "Nikki I want to hear everything. I couldn't believe the news. I wanted to call. In fact, I did call, but a police named Rocco picked up the phone and said—"

I pulled the covers closer. So nice to be cared about. "Yes I know. He told me."

"Joel Osmond shot himself in front of you at the Polo Lounge?" Lynn said in amazement.

"Yes. I had to pick up the check."

"Oh you're wicked!"

"Not as wicked as that bastard was. He was going to pin the murder of his ex-wife and her girlfriend on his own daughter."

"She must be a basket case," clucked Lynn.

"Fortunately she has her mother to console her." Beverly had really risen to the occasion after the shooting. She put her own shock aside and had Chloe move in with her, something that probably should have happened months ago. In the end, I'd bet that Beverly was even more devastated by Joel's suicide than Chloe. She'd never really stopped loving him; not that she'd ever dream of letting it show. Brooklyn.

"And that sex tape!" exclaimed Lynn. "It's everywhere."

"Poor Rita Collins. She's gone to Santa Barbara for the week."

"*TMZ* says Laci Stivers is in hiding too. And that the police have talked to her. Is she involved with the sex tape also?"

"It's a big mess, Lynn," I said as I shifted to an upright position. "The police are going to be investigating for quite a while. But if I were you, I wouldn't buy that book about how great Luna is."

"Not a good bet?"

"You're better off buying *Memoirs of a Faithful Husband* by John Edwards," I replied. Lynn laughed out loud all the way from New York.

"Well you must have been swamped by the media," she continued. "Is Piers Morgan the only show you're going to do?"

"Yes. I just wanted to set the record straight, and Piers allowed me to do that last night." Plus, every time we returned from commercial he re-introduced me as "glamorous, best-selling Hollywood novelist Nikki Tyler." You gotta love him.

"Lynn, I really thought that I should hold the rest of the interview requests for the publication of *Malibu Bad Boy*.

"Brilliant idea! In fact, love, that's just why I'm calling. Everyone's read the book, we all love it, and, in light of all the publicity from this murder case, we'd like to rush the book to market next month. If it's all right with you, that is."

I was overwhelmed. "Next month? You can really do that?"

"We've done it for presidential memoirs. And for Brittany Spears. We can do it for you."

"Then let's fire away," I declared. "I'm feeling lucky."

"Really? With Joel killing himself right in front of you and everything? I thought you might be a little rattled."

I thought back to Rocco and the good morning kiss he'd given me before heading off to the precinct. "Actually, I've been able to handle it, amazingly enough."

"That's great, Nikki. I'll be back to you in a day or so with a solid publication date and the first draft of the publicity campaign."

I hung up and pulled the covers back up to my chin. Good things were happening. There was the book and Rocco and…

Downstairs I heard the front door slam shut.

"Hey Mom? You home?"

I threw the covers off and grabbed my robe. Time to start another book.